ALWAYS A MARINE

By

I0567795

HEATHER LONG

Featuring…

Once Her Man, Always Her Man
Tell it to the Marine
Proud to Serve Her
Her Marine

ଔ

Decadent Publishing Company
www.decadentpublishing.com

This book is a work of fiction. Names, characters, places, and incidents are the products of the author's imagination or used fictitiously. Any resemblance to actual events, locales or persons, living or dead, is entirely coincidental.

Published by Decadent Publishing Company
www.decadentpublishing.com

Printed in the United States of America

~DEDICATION~

For every spouse, child, or parent who waited
for their Marine to come home.
They also serve, who stand and wait.

"What the Critics are Saying...."

Once Her Man, Always Her Man

"Hearing this author for the first time? Me too! But, being new to this author doesn't stop me from enjoying this short story. It's cool, it's great, it's hot! Whatever I say about this novel, would give the thrill away. So, for the first time in my reviewing history, there is no plot explanation...read and know for yourself. :) But, don't worry, there is some character review here instead!

Luke...Oh god, Luke! If someone can make you swoon over a man in just less than 10 minutes by talking about him, it would be Heather Long (I think). Luke is a Marine - strong, tough and charming. I hate when men play the I-hurt-you-because-I-want-to-protect-you card with the girl. But, can't help my swooning part.

Rebecca is a regular girl with a strong and kind attitude and I adore her. I am a romantic and can't help praying for Rebecca.

I forgot to say, this is erotic romance, so kids below18, please avoid this! For such a short novel, it's so good and so engaging! Would like to read more from this series." **~ Books Are Magic**

"For a quick, but totally satisfying, second-chance-at-love romance, this is the perfect choice! Sweet, touching and very sexy, this novella is a must read! And as it is short, it won't take you long to finish—even better for those times when reading a 400 page book is made almost impossible by our hectic lives! I will definitely be adding Heather Long to my list, and I look forward to seeing what one of her full-length novels has to offer. Because when she can make me fall in love with a book in less than 40 pages, imagine what she can do in 300!" **~ The Book Queen's Book Palace**

"This was such a great read. It's full of so much emotion and chemistry. You can feel the love between them, it literally jumps off the page and smacks you in the face but in such a good way. These two had a lot of hurt and pain to get through to get back to one another and I think it was done in just the right way. I'm glad I picked up this story because I really enjoyed it and I will definitely be on the lookout for more from this author." ~ **Rambling From This Chick**

Her Marine

"Lt. Brody Essex is a marine. A man of strength and honor, and maybe just the man Shannon Fabray needs. Brody wasn't looking for more than a night of passion and fun when he agreed to go on a date for an out of commission comrade in arms, but Shannon was definitely not what Brody was expecting. An exceptional woman, with her passion for life and love crushed beneath the blanket of her guilt and shame, Shannon calls to Brody's protective instincts and he vows to be the marine to bring her passion back to life, Her Marine.

I loved Brody. There is nothing better than a strong man with a soft heart. Brody was everything that Shannon needed. He seemed to "just know" the exactly right things to say and do. When to push, when to back off and when to coax. I loved how he was so willing to change his preconceived notions of the one night stand and his quiet humor.

Shannon was a great character too. I was so proud of her for attempting the one night stand and facing her fears. Watching her hesitant exploration of Brody's body and her own sexuality was like slowly opening a beautifully wrapped present from a cherished lover. Anticipation, trepidation, joy... don't rush because too soon the package will be open.

Her Marine really touched me and I will definitely be looking for the other stories in the Always a Marine series. Heather Long tells a sweet and compelling story in Her Marine and I really enjoyed her voice." ~ **Sizzling Hot Book Reviews**

Tell It To The Marine

"The third installment of Heather Long's Always a Marine series follows PFC James Westwood, Marine turned clinical psychologist so he can help out his fellow Marines acclimate to civilian life. With his whole unit signing up for the 1Night Stand service and it turning out so well for his fellow Marines, he has nothing to lose and everything to gain. Movie Star Laura Kincaid is sick of the artificial men she keeps meeting in Hollywood so she allows her agent to sign her up for 1Night Stand where she is paired up with James, who just happens to be her biggest fan. Lauren falls in love with the way he cares for his patient and fellow Marine, and he falls in love with her compassion and ability to empathize with the plight of Marines struggling to reenter civilian life.

The thing I love about the way Ms. Long tackles these Novellas is that she doesn't just cram in hot mindless sex. There is lots of hot steamy sex but she builds the story and lets us fall in love with the characters in just a short span of time. I feel like that takes a mastery that not a lot of other authors possess, and is what keeps me coming back to this series. James and Lauren aren't fully committed after one night but they are well on their way to a happily ever after, and it's believable. My biggest complaint is that story is too short, but that isn't a bad thing because it's handled beautifully, I just want more because I'm greedy and the story is that good." ~ **Harlie's Book Blog**

ONCE HER MAN, ALWAYS HER MAN

HEATHER LONG

෧

Chapter One

*L*uke Dexter handed his keys over to the red-corseted valet driver, his gaze skimming the generous globes peeking above the open buttons of her white shirt. *The Sybarite Club definitely offers the Dallas area generous access to every pleasure.* He slipped a membership card from his leather wallet and displayed it to the doorman. A tall, lanky figure dressed in topcoat and tails, the man exuded a sense of elegance that the club's exclusive clientele enjoyed.

Examining the card, he scanned it with a small device before handing it back to him. Luke admired the caginess of the action. A pen scanner would be out of place with the old world atmosphere encouraged by the man's uniform. "Good evening, Mr. Dexter. Welcome to the Sybarite Club."

He passed through the opening double wide doors. Their gothic style was dark cherry, aged like a fine wine and decorated with wood cut carvings of a man and woman engaged in cunnilingus and fellatio. The subtle joining left each crying out in pleasure when the door opened, only to be reunited when the doors closed.

Amused by the art, he smiled before plunging into the velvet darkness of the club's jazz-infused atmosphere. Every night featured a different style of music, but Fridays were reserved for jazz. Old world, cool, smooth music with smoky voices, haunting guitars and lonely horns played to the soul. The doors barely closed behind him when his phone buzzed.

Pulling it out, he thumbed it on. A new message from Madame Evangeline of the 1Night Stand dating service populated the screen. *She's dressed in green silk and sitting at the bar. Remember, Luke, life doesn't always offer a second chance....*

Clicking the screen off, he walked down the four red-carpeted steps into the lounge proper. He'd only agreed to the dating service in a show of solidarity with the men in his unit. Many of his men continued to struggle with reintegration and forming new relationships. He couldn't excuse himself from that same issue or the expected invitation to the Sybarite Club. His gaze roamed the room, coming to a halt and fastening on a pair of to-die-for tan legs at the bar. The sweet length of them, one crossed over the other and ended in black heels with crystals glittering around dainty feet.

A green skirt skimmed her knees. He studied the line of her back, curious about the rest of her. His gaze slid higher to the pile of unruly auburn hair fighting to escape a pair of crystal hair combs.

As though sensing his appraisal, the mystery woman turned on the bar stool and his heart tripped.

Rebecca....

೮3

Eleven years earlier....

She raced across the field, the sunrise illuminating auburn hair streaming behind her. Luke paused, football helmet in hand. His heart squeezed every time he saw her. He'd known her since kindergarten, dated her since the day she'd turned sixteen and now in the autumn of their senior year, he couldn't believe she still showed up two hours early for school every morning just to watch him practice and eat breakfast with him.

The guys razzed him about being whipped, but he ignored their ribbing. After all, *he* had Rebecca. He opened his arms and braced himself for the crushing hug as she wrapped her arms and legs around him. He adored her enthusiastic greetings. He'd adore them more if he weren't battered, bruised and battened down in football pads.

"Good morning!" She kissed him, simple, sweet and sensational.

"G'morning, sunshine." He chuckled, nuzzling the corner of her mouth and the scrape of sugar that alerted him to powdered donuts for breakfast. His heart squeezed again. Powdered donuts were his favorite, but he had a strict diet during the season, a diet that she managed to add at least one powdered donut meal to per week.

Two of the new guys catcalled, but his co-captain, Brent, shoved the whistlers onward to follow the rest of the team. After a year of her openly affectionate displays, the team was used to Lowell High's lovebirds.

She waved to Brent and leaned back, tilting her head toward Luke. "You didn't get a lot of sleep last night."

"History paper," he sighed. "Really couldn't give a damn about the Archduke Franz Ferdinand, but Mr. Paulette didn't ask for my opinion."

"Only the facts, Mr. Dexter, or take a seat and zip it." She dropped her voice an octave, mimicking their world history teacher. Her perfect white teeth bit her lower lip. "Want me to read it over while you practice?"

"Yes, I'm not too proud to admit it, either. It's in my backpack." Setting her down, he carefully avoided giving her rump a good squeeze. As affectionate as she was, she had boundaries. Explicit boundaries he respected. No sex in private or carnal petting in public. Of course, that didn't stop him from looking at her perfect heart-shaped rear. She always complained about her weight and wanted to lose ten pounds.

He really had no idea why, either. Curvy as hell, she filled out her shirts and jeans beautifully and he loved wrapping his arms around her. She felt real against him. The one time he'd gotten her shirt off, he'd gaped at the sweet roundness of her breasts peeking out over the simple white bra. Her nipples stiffened under the fabric, dark and dusky. He'd damn near choked on his own drool at the thought of being able to touch them with his lips.

Maybe after homecoming.

"What are you thinking about?" She set her bag down on the riser next to his.

"You." He admitted. "Naked."

She laughed. "You need to think about your end zone and running backs and whatever it is they were doing that got you tackled yesterday."

And her lack of knowledge about football never stopped her from coming to practice and showing up at every game, even the away ones, to cheer him on. When they'd made divisional the previous year, only strep throat kept her home. Worried about her, he'd sucked hard during that game.

"Yeah, but I don't want to think about their butts or how they look naked."

Her cheeks pinkened, a ripe, sweet color and his heart jerked and shook like a dog with a toy.

The coach whistled, done with their dawdling.

"See you in an hour?"

"I'll be right here." She pointed at the risers. "Reading your paper."

"Love you." His voice dropped, not because it embarrassed him to say it or worried that someone might overhear, but because loving Rebecca was a privilege, *his* privilege and he sure as shit didn't plan on sharing it with the team.

"I love you, too." She mouthed the words, but they drove right into him and lit his insides. Her love honored him. Blowing him a kiss, she shooed him away. He jogged out to meet the team, sure she kept his heart as safe and sound as his homework.

ଔ

"Rebecca." He barely managed to mouth her name. Just like that, the jaunt in his step faltered, his heart stuttered and he half-turned to head back out the door. The valet probably hadn't even parked his car yet.

That's the coward's way out.

Luke Dexter wasn't a coward.

Not anymore.

He thought back to the all-too-knowing text message. *Life doesn't always offer a second chance....*

Walk out the door and run away—again—or walk across the floor of the Sybarite and take his chance?

I'm through running.

Rebecca Rainier glanced at her watch. She'd had some crazy clients over the years, but Delilah Swanson had to be the most eccentric. Becca began her event planning business in college and *Rainier's Intimate Introductions* catered to the concept that people needed intimate situations to celebrate, meet, and mark special moments in their lives. She'd split her time between classes and meetings, carrying her supplies, her notes and her files around in the trunk of her car.

After graduation, Delilah made her an offer. She forwarded the financing for a storefront, let Rebecca choose her own clients, save for the once a year soiree Delilah hosted for a handpicked guest list. The ideal silent partner, she maintained a tidy investment, even after Rebecca paid off the initial stake.

For five years, she did exactly as she pleased, planning birthday parties, welcome home parties, wakes, weddings, and everything in between. This year's grand shindig for Delilah sent Becca to the Sybarite Club in Dallas, only a few miles from where she'd grown up.

If it had been anyone else, she would have said no. But Delilah insisted that no life outside of work would impact her career more than she could imagine, so she'd let her not-so-silent partner sign her up for the 1Night Stand dating service. Delilah chose the Sybarite Club for the meeting, she knew the guys who ran it and that guaranteed her a measure of security. Instead of a huge party on some far-flung island or cruise ship, she waited for the man of the hour.

Delilah's text had been specific: *The Sybarite Club, nine PM., wear a forest green dress.* She'd even sent a silver bracelet for her to wear for luck and love. The simple band shackling her wrist was heavier than most of the pieces she favored, but its weight comforted and warmed her.

A mournful melody of horn, piano and guitar tugged her back from the past—a place she rarely ventured anymore. She'd give her partner's crazy idea another half hour. The white wine, the intimate atmosphere and the jazz were certainly worth another half hour of her time.

Maybe the guy chickened out.

Sadly, it wouldn't be the first time.

A delicious scent of woodsy vanilla stroked across her senses, locking every muscle in her body. Tension knitted a chain of knots up her spine. Trembling, she set the wine glass down before spilling it. The scent teased her, conjuring memories of high school, football and love. Tears clogged her throat, and the colorful collection of liquors on the bar back rippled as the curtain shrouding her heart ripping away.

Luke....

❃

Eleven years earlier

"I don't understand." She sat on the edge of the picnic table. Instead of the movies, they'd planned a quiet Saturday night together. But he'd been late and just when she thought he wouldn't show up, he'd arrived, agitated, out of sorts and distant. "What happened?"

"September 11th happened, Becca. We're retaliating and I plan to help." The sweet autumn of their graduating year had turned into a nightmare a few weeks before. She'd been with him when the first reports of the terrorist attacks came in. School dismissed early, but not early enough to stop the news of the flight numbers involved. His mother and sister had been on a flight out of Dulles that morning, returning home from touring colleges on the east coast.

He'd taken the news without a glimmer of emotion. Her heart ached for him. For weeks, he pressed through funerals, obligatory family visits and bore the brunt of the hushed pity that rippled through the halls of Lowell High wherever they went.

He quit the football team.

His grades slipped.

He stopped coming to school regularly.

But Rebecca hadn't left him. She brought his homework, bullied him to eat, cleaned up after both he and his father. After 9/11, his retired Marine, Navy reservist father informed them over dinner that he'd been activated. She held Luke's hand through his father's speech.

"Dad's leaving tomorrow. He reports to Camp Pendleton. I'm going with him." His words struck her like a body blow.

They're moving. A hell of a long way from Lowell High School and Rockwall, Texas.

"Luke...." She squeezed his hand. The chill icing her heart suffocated the unseasonably warm Christmas air. "Wait."

He'd avoided direct eye contact since walking up to the picnic table and he'd been stiff when she'd hugged him. He looked at her then, and it wasn't her Luke, but a stranger, cool and remote. "I'm not sorry. And I'm not going just because Dad got called up. I enlisted in the Marines yesterday."

I enlisted.... The words knocked around like a silver pinball caught bouncing between two objects, pinging against her soul. *Enlisted in what?*

"I'm eighteen. I took my GED this morning. Dad has some pull, so basic starts the week after Christmas. I don't have to wait."

Confusion added a second ball pinging around with the first. *Luke enlisted. He joined the Marines.* "When did you...?"

"Last month, after my birthday. Dad drove me down to...." His words drifted away, muted by the static in her brain. "...and that's that. You're great, but you've already gotten your acceptance letters to Brown and you're going to school."

"You're breaking up with me?" She hadn't meant to blurt it out, but shock cut off her good sense.

"Becca, America is going to retaliate. We're already going into Afghanistan, and if I can get done with basic fast enough, I'll be going with them. Bin Laden needs to die for what he did. Those fanatics need to understand that they attacked us. We have a duty to defend our country, to speak up for everyone who died."

"Luke, I know. I know how you feel."

"No." He pulled his hand out from under hers. "You don't know how I feel. And I don't want you to ever know how I feel about this. A clean break is better. You're great. Some guy is going to snap you right up and you're going to have a great future. It'll be easier on both of us if we make it a clean break now. I don't want you to have to wait, to worry or to wonder."

Nothing she said after that got through. He'd made up his mind. He'd taken her home, not even kissing her as he left her on the sidewalk in front of her house. He wasn't home the next day.

Or the day after that.

A week later, the Dexter house had a For Sale sign in front of it.

A month later, a new family moved into it.

Rebecca didn't know where he'd gone, so she addressed her letters to both he and his father, in care of the Marines.

She wrote him weekly.

Studying any news reports coming out of Afghanistan, she was terrified that one day they'd include a tidbit: *local Rockwall boy dies overseas.*

She didn't go to Brown, sticking it out at the University of North Texas and commuting. She wanted to be where he'd left her.

So he could find her again.

A week before she graduated, an email blast from their high school graduating class's annual newsletter caught her eye. Lieutenant Luke Dexter, former Lowell High football star, had been awarded a medal for bravery in combat. He remained on assignment in Afghanistan after a brief visit to speak at the school.

A brief visit.
He had come home.
But he hadn't called.
She never sent him another letter.

☙

Her chest squeezed unbearably tight at the scent, the woodsy vanilla as familiar to her as her own skin. She'd never forgotten how he smelled. Even now, the rich warmth of it rolled over her, carrying her back to more carefree days—breakfast at the football field, late afternoons lying in a tangle, trying to study. Long, wet, tongue-stroking kisses.

Painful cracks spider-webbed across the ancient headstone burying her heart. She'd mourned him and stopped visiting him in her heart a long time ago. The scent dragged the roots of her teenage passion, screaming and clawing, out from under the debris of years.

"Rebecca." His voice washed over her and she closed her eyes. *It can't be him.*

Not now.

She didn't turn. She couldn't. She squeezed her eyes shut, closing out the abandoned seventeen-year old girl who'd dared to hope, pray and dream that one day he would reach out to her again. Let her be there.

Instead, the twenty-eight-year old woman shook off a teenage melodramatic gasp and forced her eyes back open, glancing toward the mirror behind the bar. Hooded, hazel eyes met hers and her heart belly flopped, pain smashing through every nerve.

Chapter Two

Luke's chest hurt, but he braced himself against it. Shock wrinkled the line between her brows, the emotion far more brutal to him than a firefight in Kandahar or Kabul. She didn't turn to look at him. But her reflection in the mirror didn't soften. The familiar, flirtatious smile fled from the cool, firm line of her lips. Color drained from the face of the woman who shifted on the bar stool. Movement to his right caught his attention. A man approached, intent on her, but meeting Luke's iron expression, the would-be interloper diverted to another table.

Satisfied, his attention returned to the girl—no, the woman— gazing at him, pain etching the softness of her lips. The memory of her lips got him through Parris Island. He'd thought about them, about her smile, every single, damn day.

"Hello, Luke." Her voice poured over him like warm honey.

Life doesn't always offer second chances....

"May I join you?" He nodded to the stool next to her.

"It's a free country." And just like that, she turned her back and the warm honey chilled, hardening over his chest.

"Thank you, ma'am." He tacked the ma'am on as an afterthought. But the steel wrapped in her velvety voice jabbed his kidneys. Perching on the edge of the stool, he motioned to the bartender. "Two more of whatever the lady is having."

She watched him from the mirror. Hungriness reflected in the

19

gold flecked, tawny brown eyes, a perfect contrast to the tight jaw and stiff fingers wrapped around her wine glass. She tossed back a third of a glass like a shot of vodka.

A shot of vodka sounded like a great idea. But he needed his wits about him. IEDs laced the battlefield in front of him and patience and procedure and about eighty-five pounds of protective gear weren't handy. But the trick to survival was to examine what was right in front of him and to react to it. He could do that in the field, he could do that with her. It was what he did best.

After the bartender served the drinks and took his credit card, Luke shifted to sit sideways, intentionally brushing his leg against hers. She didn't recoil—exactly—but did shift away after a few seconds. *Definitely treading in dangerous waters.*

"How are you?" Lame, but it beat the first thing that came to mind. Dragging her off the icy perch and kissing her until she became that soft, warm, dewy-eyed girl he remembered wouldn't go well. He ignored that savage need.

For now.

"I was sorry to hear about your father." The words brushed over him, smoothing away the long years stretching between them.

"He died exactly as he intended." Luke had no illusions. *Not anymore.* His father had been a Marine through and through. After their family loss, he returned to the Corps with a vengeance. He stopped being Dad and simply became Sir. His work in Afghanistan and Iraq saved a lot of lives, but a roadside bomber claimed him. The old man was at peace, hopefully with Luke's mom and Brianna.

"You didn't go to the funeral." Every inflection carefully measured, she cradled the wine glass and avoided looking at him directly, watching via the mirror instead—a distancing technique—the PSYOP guys would love her. The modulated tone and her expression created a cocktail of distance and intimacy that left the listener eager to bridge the empty spaces.

"I was still overseas. I wasn't aware there was much of a

funeral." *Had she gone? Had she gone hoping to see me?* He could have returned for the it, but a near miss on a personal assignment left him laid up for six weeks and the doctors wouldn't let him fly.

"Mrs. Carter hosted a wake, and half of Rockwall attended the funeral." Irritation crept into her words. "Protestors posted that they planned to demonstrate. Bastards. So the Carters and the Phelps called home everyone who could make it."

The town showed up to protect his dad. Something heavy shifted off Luke's heart. Rebecca showed up to protect his dad. The armed forces defended the rights of the people including those protesting. They didn't like the protestors, but they'd been trained to ignore them and let them exercise their God-given freedoms.

"Thank you." Her words echoed through him. "Dad would have appreciated it."

She nodded, clearly done with speaking. The silence stretched taut between them. He considered all the angles. A loss for words was not a familiar handicap.

"Rebecca."

"Why are you here, Luke?" She turned then, the full force of her gaze striking him. Nothing prepared him for *her*, the woman, poised, self-possessed and prettier than a runway model. Her head tilted to the side, she stared at him openly. He leaned forward, closing the distance between them. Once upon a time, he could boast no secrets existed between them because her shining face echoed every thought, every emotion. But that book was closed to him. He couldn't tell what feelings raced through her, whether happy, sad, or terrifyingly indifferent to seeing him.

"I came home."

Surprise skittered across her face, cracking the indifferent veneer. Another stone slid away from his heart. Maybe she hadn't realized it yet, but she *was* happy to see him. And a little upset. But he could work with both.

"Not to Rockwall, I would have heard if you'd moved home." No artifice existed in those words. They'd grown up in Rockwall's bedroom community long before the superhighways extended their reach and the franchises moved in. Their tight neighborhood and Lowell still sent out a newsletter to graduates every year.

He relied on those dribs and drabs of information to keep up with her. She'd graduated from the University of North Texas with a 4.0 and offers from multi-billion dollar corporations. She hosted movie stars at her parties in Texas and around the world. The glamorous graduate never released any information about her personal life, just her success. *But is she in love or happy?*

"No, not to Rockwall," he agreed easily, shifting until he set a foot on the bottom of her stool, caging her away from the rest of the bar. The smoky jazz, the hushed atmosphere, even the bartender chatting up some regulars faded away. She passed the wine glass from her left hand to her right and set it down.

His gaze zeroed in on the left hand.

No ring.

No line where a ring might have been.

A third rock tumbled away, unearthing his heart from the tomb he'd locked it away in.

"No, not Rockwall. Allen. I had a house built there. I'm opening a rehabilitation center not far from the Village at Allen, specializing in psychiatric and physical disorders for veterans." The longest string of words he'd managed since seeing her in the bar, but he could talk about Mike's Place all day.

"Mike's Place. You're opening Mike's Place?" Interest surged in Rebecca's voice.

"You've heard of it?" They'd netted a fair piece of media attention, but the doors weren't open yet.

"I'm planning the opening gala in three weeks."

"We have a company hosting that gala. You work for Intimate Introductions?"

"I own it."

And just like that, the blocks of information tumbled into place. The company's representatives had taken a huge interest in Mike's Place, including a prospective fundraiser for the physical therapy wing. The promised funds allowed him to put more of his resources into other areas. James Westwood from his unit had already put him in touch with more than a dozen solid therapists, all with military backgrounds, who'd leapt eagerly at the chance to work with their own, even those who'd be picking up sticks and moving cross country to set up shop in Allen, Texas.

His Rebecca owned Intimate Introductions.

He owed the lady at 1Night Stand a bottle of wine and a box of chocolates.

"I had no idea you were involved with Mike's Place." Her voice dropped to a hoarse whisper, setting off the warning bells in his head. He jerked his attention back to her as she slid off the stool, away from him. "I'm sorry. I'll have my assistant manage the onsite coordination. You won't have to see me."

Won't have to see her....

"I'm glad things are going well for you, Luke. It was good to see you again." A tight smile betrayed anything but and then she walked away, her too-tall heels clicking against the floor like nails being driven into the coffin he'd just busted out of.

The hell she's walking away.

He tossed a couple of bills on the bar and strode after her. He caught up to her at the curb and handed a hundred to the girl she gave her claim check to. "My car, not hers."

"Excuse me?" Rebecca wheeled around, but not before he saw her wiping away glittering tears from her eyes.

"My car. Not yours." His heart constricted. He'd made her cry and that made him the lowest form of life. He'd have to take himself out back to get the shit kicked out of him for that. He knew a couple of guys who'd help him out.

Later.

"You can't just order me around, Luke." The wash of tears thickening her voice evaporated in a blast of anger.

"I didn't order you around. I ordered her." He nodded toward the valet who'd already disappeared with his money. Rebecca's sweet mouth rounded into a silent O and he grinned. That was his girl, emotions running riot across the smooth, pristine face. Anger, irritation, sadness and yes, lust, all paraded through her expression. As if aware of his delight, she faced away, her shoulders stiff and jerky.

"That's semantics."

"No, that's fact. I've never given you an order."

"No, you just took the choice out of my hands." She folded her arms across her chest, a shiver trembling through her tight frame. Shrugging out of his suit jacket, he draped it around her, closing his hands on her shoulders when she would have pulled away.

"You're cold. It's a jacket. It won't bite." He carefully measured the words, savoring the feeling of her under his hands although touching her had been a mistake. He didn't want to stop.

The valet pulled his F450 into the slip in front of the Sybarite Club. The engine idled as she stepped out. He circled Rebecca, keeping one hand on her shoulder in case she tried to dart away again. He opened the passenger door and dared a look at her.

The pain and confusion shimmering in her eyes strangled him. *I really do need to have my ass kicked.*

"What do you want?"

"I want you to come with me and I want to apologize." Honest, straightforward and not shying away from the problem. He could take the well-deserved lumps, but she didn't deserve them. He'd done her a huge disservice. Time to put that right.

Long past time.

"Will you come with me?" Careful not to give her an order, not to push too hard, not to force a retreat.

"Why?"

"Because I won't leave you behind this time...." *I won't leave you behind ever again.*

She hesitated. "My car is here."

"When you want to come back, I'll bring you back."

White teeth pulled at her lower lip, clearly conflicted.

"Becca, I don't deserve the chance, but I need one. Just one. Please."

She dropped her gaze. Luke held his breath. He wasn't above begging. Not for her.

"Okay."

He barely heard her too-quiet reply, and remained uncertain he heard the answer correctly until she took a step toward the truck. "I'll go."

He handed her up into the truck, careful to watch that she didn't turn an ankle in the insane stilettos, no matter how great they made her legs look. Shutting the door behind her, he caught the doorman's bemused expression. The man nodded his head, mouthing *good luck.*

Luke nodded in return, taking it.

He needed all the luck he managed to bank over the years and then some. He'd left her once, but this Marine didn't make the same mistake twice. And he knew where to go. Leaving Dallas on I-30, he headed for Rockwall.

Chapter Three

*T*he vents blasted a blanket of warmth into the silence, but the heat couldn't quite touch the icy core solidifying in her chest. She sat next to a stranger. No, she sat next to Luke, far *worse* than a stranger. She didn't know what to say. Her tongue seemed thick against the back of her teeth.

Two glasses of wine left her mildly tipsy. The only explanation for why she got into the truck with the man eleven years after he walked away and never looked back. *Stupid, stupid, childish mistake. You're not seventeen anymore, Becca.*

At twenty-eight, she had no excuses for bad choices.

"Better?"

"What?" She pulled away from her internal monologue to stare across the shadowy gulf to the man driving.

"Are you warmer?" His voice gentled and she wished he'd stop doing that. Stop sounding like the boy who used to carry her over muddy spots rather than risk her slipping, or the guy who listened intently to every critique she gave him on his homework, or the sweet boyfriend who grinned like an idiot when she raced up to hug him.

She'd *missed* that boy for years.

"I'm fine." She licked her lips. *This is a bad idea. Why now? Why tonight?* Why had Delilah cajoled her into changing her schedule so that she would spend the winter in Dallas rather than

Dubai, to plan an event for Mike's Place rather than an oil tycoon? *Did she know? I told her about Luke, but did she realize they were the same man before she set this up?*

"Why Mike's Place?"

If the question surprised him, he didn't show it. In fact, he looked very relaxed leaning back in the seat, his right hand resting on the steering wheel. Sliding her heels off, she shifted to tuck one leg over the other. The damn shoes cost a fortune and pinched her toes.

"I've seen what back to back wars do to the men and women who serve, and their families. Mothers who don't see their kids for years. Fathers who return, a wad of stress and out of sorts. Soldiers who can't reintegrate because their personal worlds moved on without them, and the injured who are struggling to figure out who they are now without an arm, a leg or the ability to walk. It's a bitch and we don't leave people behind, especially when they come home. Mike's Place will provide the lodestone for a lot of lives."

Tears misted across her vision. She'd poured over the literature for Mike's Place, the thirty-acre complex providing physical therapy centers, mental health pavilions, free clinic services and a childcare facility. Donations requested, but not required, covered the near non-existent cost to patients. Out-of-state visitors would be provided with access to onsite apartments for both patient and family.

"It's a beautiful idea." She whispered the words and it *was*. Thoughtful, generous and compassionate. Just like the boy she'd loved. He had been Lowell High's best football player. Even the year he'd left the team to enter the military, he'd been nominated for MVP. Not for being best player on the field, but rather because Luke took the concept of, *no I in team,* to the extreme.

Oh, I've missed him so much.

Missed him, past tense, not present. She tugged her gaze away from his profile lest the naked need running rampant through her shine on her face. Every man she'd dared to date had to live up to the ghost of his estimation.

None had passed.

"Thanks." A note of shyness slipped into his deep voice. "It's good work. It needs to be done."

Rebecca rubbed two fingers carefully under one eye, sweeping away the tears that kept trying to slip free. "Who's Mike?"

It was Luke's turn to sigh. The poignant note pulled her gaze back. The highway's interspersed lights strobed across his profile, revealing a raw emotion that had her hand reaching out to rest on his arm. He covered her slender hand with his own, trapping her there, but she didn't care. Pain echoed through him and he needed her.

"Mike Nowiski went through basic with me. Two years older than me, he'd dropped out of college to enlist. He grew up in New Jersey. His parents owned a pizza joint, and he married his high school sweetheart for love. They had a baby girl, just a year old when Mike enlisted. He was a good guy, never shut up about his kid. He joked that the Marines would give him all the know-how he needed to cap any punk who wanted to date her. I met his wife, twice. Shari was a sweetheart. They had that real thing, crazy in love, but supportive as hell. She was amazing, we spent four years in Afghanistan, and Mike never had leave to go home except for one seventy-two hour furlough. Shari flew to meet him halfway in Germany."

Dread curled around Rebecca's heart. So many of Luke's words were past tense, not present. But she squeezed his arm, the heat of his bicep melting the ice chips on her soul.

"Three years ago, Mike got injured. We were in Iraq, monitoring a school rebuild. Insurgents tossed a few grenades, brought down most of the unfinished building. Mike took shrapnel in the leg helping the workers get out. It was bad. They airlifted him to Germany, and he spent ten weeks getting pins in his leg to rebuild it. Then they sent him home."

Fear squeezing her heart, she waited. A muscle ticked in his jaw and they were gliding down the exit ramp. He took a left at the light and blended in with the evening traffic. Lights from the strip malls illuminated the truck, reflecting off his angry, tortured visage.

"What happened, Luke?" She couldn't stand the silence.

"Three weeks after he got home, he shot Shari and then himself. The reports said he suffered from severe PTSD. Shari had spoken to a chaplain about his violent mood swings and nightmares, but the day before the chaplain's scheduled visit, something in Mike snapped. He was a good man, he *loved* his wife. What happened to him overseas, the war, the injury, changed him and he didn't get the support services he needed. I know he shot himself because he killed Shari, but it doesn't change the fact that his little girl is now an orphan. She's barely eleven and she has no one, no family. Mike's Place can't save everyone, but kids like Amy Nowiski shouldn't have to bury their parents, and guys like Mike should have a place to go to get better while women like Shari have the support they need to be there for their spouse."

Her tears fell freely at his words. *What a horrible story.* "You should tell people Mike's story," she sniffled. Damn it, she'd always been a crier and the flow of damp grief stung her eyes. "You should tell them Shari's story and Amy's story. It's terrible, but it makes it more real for those who can't imagine what that's like."

"Aww, hell, Becca, I didn't mean to make you cry." His grief stricken expression dissolved in self-recrimination. He shifted to put his left hand on the wheel, his right capturing hers and lifting it to his lips. The tender brush of a kiss across her knuckles damn near brought her to sobbing.

"I can't help it. You miss Mike. You're pissed at yourself because Mike went home and you weren't there to watch his back, to protect his family and save him from himself. But it's not your fault." The words hiccupped, but she didn't care. He swung the truck into a dark parking lot and shifted into park before twisting in the seat.

Between one breath and the next, he'd snapped off her seat belt and tugged her across the bench until she crushed up against him. It was a mistake to hold him like that, to let him hold her. But he needed her.

Hell, I need him.

She sobbed all over his nice dress shirt. Her arms slid around him, her hands going to his hair. Still cut high and tight, she missed the gentler waves where it would tumble in his eyes. He'd come back a bigger, harder man, but cocooned against him, the years slipped away.

A rumble shook through him, a low laugh tickled her and the bubble of tension inside her popped. Laughing through tears was the best emotion and the more he laughed against her, the more laughter punctuated her tears.

"Why are you laughing?" She chuckled, pulling back enough to look at him. But the circle of his arms trapped her close. His forehead drifted down to rest against hers, his eyes dark and unfathomable in the next to nothing light.

"This is so not what I meant when I asked you to come with me. I never wanted you to cry."

She shrugged, no easy feat this close when it brushed her chest to his and her nipples stiffened. A lazy thread of desire unwound from the tension, zinging along half-forgotten nerve endings. Eleven years and his proximity still turned her on.

Who am I kidding? She'd loved this man her whole life. When he asked her out on a date the day of her sixteenth birthday party, she'd written in her diary that she'd been born to love him. Eleven years and heartbreak didn't diminish the feeling no matter how much hurt and resentment she'd tried to bury it in.

"Luke," she whispered. "I'm glad you're here. I'm glad you told me. I've missed you."

He went still against her. She shoved away the regret that crept through her. She would never regret reaching out to him. It hurt to think he might reject her.

Again.

But she would never stop being there. He spoke of Shari in wonder, wonder for how she supported the man she loved, wonder for how she managed all those years and would be willing to fly halfway around the world for a couple of days, but she didn't wonder.

I would have done the same damn thing if he'd just let me.

Resolve exploded through her, she was through waiting for him to give her that opportunity. Nestled close to him, the warmth of his breath tickling her cheek, and the strength of his arms around her, she closed the gap to press her lips to his.

He stiffened, but his mouth opened to her questing tongue. The gentle kiss went from zero to raging forest fire. Liquid heat blasted through her blood and between one breath and the next, she straddled his lap, his hands pulling her hair loose to tumble down around them in a curtain. Every inch of his hard muscle pressed against her softer flesh. He tasted of the wine he'd ordered at Sybarite and something darker, deeper and more masculine.

He tastes like Luke.

A groan rolled through her as his tongue sought entry, dueling with hers, stroking her teeth, lapping up every breath. Her dress inched up her thighs and the hard length of his cock burned through the clothes separating them. She rolled her hips, rubbing against him, sending tingles of electricity darting through her sex.

She soaked her panties at the thought of stripping away those last barriers. She wanted to feel him inside of her. They'd played it safe for years, never even made it past second base.

"Rebecca," his voice slurred ever so slightly between kisses as their mouths moved together. It was like dancing, tongues waltzing together, circling each other. "Rebecca."

He leaned his head back, fingers fisting in her hair, trapping her when she would have followed. His chest rose and fell. His excitement fueled her own. "Sweetheart, you're killing me." His murmur was low and throaty. Would he sound that raspy and hoarse when they were naked and rolling together? She shuddered, one aching tangle of need. Her body vibrated with it. Her hands flattened against his chest, the pounding of his heart a delicious cadence beneath her questing fingers as she unbuttoned his shirt.

"I don't think it's ever hurt this good," she murmured. She

wanted to feel his skin, to see his body, to touch every inch of him with her hands and her mouth. He covered her hands with one of his, halting her action.

"Becca, stop." The order shuddered through the desire questing in her system.

"You don't want me?" The traitorous words slipped out before she could stop them. Even in the low light cast by the dashboard, she saw the words strike their mark.

"Baby, I want you more than I can say. But not like this, not because you're feeling sorry for me."

He couldn't have cooled her ardor faster if he'd slapped her. "Sorry for you?" She repeated the words, hardly believing them. "Sorry for you?"

"Becca...." His tone shifted, wary. She tore away, ignoring her body's lonely cry as she tumbled onto the passenger seat. She grabbed the door handle and jerked it open, all but falling out of the truck.

He was out the driver's side door and circling around even as she found her shoes and her purse. The cold night air provided the bracing reality check she needed against the wild desire riding hard through her body.

"Becca, wait."

"The hell I will." Fury pounded in her temples, mingling with her aggravated desire and frustrated need. "That wasn't feeling sorry for you, you...you...jerk." She punched her finger at his chest. "That was me loving you." He took one step back as her finger jabbed him again. "That was me reaching out to you."

Another jab. Another step back.

"That was me wanting you." She jabbed him one more time. "I have never felt sorry for you. I grieved with you. I hurt with you. I missed you until I thought my heart would wither and die. But I have never pitied you."

She whirled, fueled by eleven years of loneliness and betrayal. She had no idea where the hell they'd parked, but she couldn't stay there. *Not for this.* Not when her love bled like a raw wound, the stitches she'd knitted around her broken heart tearing loose.

"Becca, I love you."

And now he has to go and say that.

Chapter Four

*L*uke clenched his fists, forcing himself to wait. If he touched her again, they would be in the bed of his truck and he'd be driving away all his good intentions as he thrust into her hot, sweet, willing body. He'd called himself a fool for stopping her. The first, sweet taste of her lips in over a decade, and time turned back to high school.

No, not high school—home.

Home. For the first time since he walked out of the damn park, he'd come home. Too much between them to not do this right, to not answer the questions that he'd left burning between them.

No way would he walk away this time, but she deserved every opportunity he'd denied her. Her fury was a beautiful thing. Her swollen lips glistened, her face flushed, and her eyes sparked. His radiant Rebecca, so righteous in her fury.

"Babe, I love you." He repeated slowly, watching the slim line of the back she'd turned on him. Again. He knew every inch of her, not as intimately as he might like, but he used to be an expert in her expressions, body language, and soul. He might be rusty, but he trusted his instincts. She didn't run.

Not now.

"What do you want from me?" Pain wrenched through every word.

It's now or never, Dexter. Man up, Marine.

"I want to tell you about the worst day of my life." Not an eloquent man, he couldn't even pretend. But Becca needed truth. She needed honesty. If it hurt him, then he deserved the stripes on his soul for every injury, real or imagined, he'd inflicted on her.

The park had been redubbed President George Bush Park in 2005, but it would always be Preston Park to him. Still the place he met his girlfriend to break her heart.

And mine.

Her shoulders lifted, her head tilted upward. She sucked in a noisy breath of air, exasperation taut in the expression she turned back toward him. Standing there, stocking feet on the hard asphalt, spiky heels in one hand, purse in the other, rumpled dress, and disheveled hair, she seemed both patient and pissed.

God, I love her.

"I'm listening." If that was the best she had to offer, he'd take it.

"Get back in the truck so you're not cold?" He tacked the question mark on as an afterthought, but when her eyebrows rose, he backed off. He could warm her feet up when they finished.

"Mom died. Brianna died. Dad went away. I was pissed. Angrier than I've ever been about anything. I wanted to do something about it. The Marines offered me a way to not only avenge them, but to honor them, too. I can't even tell you when the idea entered my head." He fought for neutrality. He didn't like explaining himself to anyone. *But she isn't just anyone, she's the only one.*

"I told Dad I wanted to apply and he drove me down to the recruiter. I talked to the guy for an hour and then I signed the papers. I applied for my GED the same day. I wanted to talk to you about it, but I thought it wasn't fair to you to put that decision on your plate. I didn't think it was right that I was taking your last year of high school down the drain with mine. I couldn't protect Mom or Brianna, but I could protect you."

He dared to look at her and the haughty distance in her expression melted. "You didn't have to protect me...."

"The hell I didn't. You were putting everything on hold to look after us. You were at the house every night, cooking dinner, sitting with Dad. Hell, you were even doing the laundry. You were my sanctuary and I wanted to lose myself with you, but if I'd told you I was going, you would have supported it, packed me up and waited. Sat here, waiting for me." He dared her to disagree with him. But the mutinous expression answered without words. Yes, she would have waited, and he wouldn't have stopped thinking about her.

"But babe, before you start hating me for not wanting you to wait for me, that wasn't it...that wasn't it at all. I wanted to marry you, I wanted to fill you with babies, but I was an eighteen- year old kid with a GED and a hate on for Al Qaida, heading off to the Marines where I was pretty sure I was going to get myself busted up. I wanted *more* for you than that."

"You are such an idiot." She flung her shoes down and he counted himself lucky she didn't throw them at him. He took a step forward, edging back into her space.

"Yes, I was. But I was a kid. A kid who was stupid in love. A kid who would have been stupid if all I ever thought about was you. If you were here, I didn't think I could leave you. Making you hate me was the coward's way out, but I thought you would be better off, you could meet a guy, marry him, have a dozen babies." Bile crawled up his throat at the idea of some other guy touching her, holding her, loving her. Worse, the sourness at the idea that she might love this faceless, nameless bastard that Luke would have throttled.

"So it was easier to just dump me? To walk away? To say nothing?"

"Yeah. After, I couldn't take it back. Then your letters came."

Her sharp, indrawn breath stabbed him in the gut. "You got them."

"I have every single one that you wrote." The first one arrived while at basic—the flowing script cutting him. He'd worn away the return address on the first one, stroking a thumb over it. "But I couldn't open them. I had to make the break clean."

"Why? Why would it have been so awful to know I was here for you? That I would wait, support you in any way I could? Why wouldn't you let me be there for you?" She took a step toward him.

"Because I was scared, Becca. Scared that I'd get out there and the only thing I would do is think about you, get killed, and leave you grieving. At least, I told myself, if I did buy it over there, you wouldn't be mourning me. You'd have a great life and it was all I had to give then."

If he could go back to his eighteen-year-old self, he'd thump him hard. His dad even agreed with his decision, but in retrospect, his father didn't see much point to civilian life and love anymore. He turned all Marine, all the time, after their loss.

"But I kept the letters. When I deployed, my base commander kept them and shipped them over in bulk. They went everywhere with me. I promised myself when I came home for good, I'd read them then. I'd read them and see the life you'd built for yourself."

"And have you?" She stood directly in front of him then, staring up at him, tears shimmering in her eyes.

"Nope. I wanted to, but I had the idea for Mike's Place and I guess I came back here because I wanted to be close to you. Told myself I'd get Mike's Place started and then I'd read them."

"You were never going to read them, Luke Dexter." Exasperated amusement, not censure, filtered through her words.

"I'm an ass, Becca. I'm an ass who loved you too much to hold onto you. But I'm not ass enough to walk away this time. I'm right here. I'll do whatever penance you want, I'll get on my knees if you need me too, and I'll crawl the rest of my life if that's what it takes to prove it to you." The text-messaged words echoed in his mind. They were the right words. "Life doesn't always offer second chances and I sure as sh—heck don't deserve one, but...."

He hesitated. He wasn't pleading his case really well. Hell, he didn't even know if she had some jackass in her life. He considered the way she'd crawled into his lap and the lack of ring on her finger and he'd bet he could push the imaginary boyfriend out without a hell of a lot of effort.

Rebecca blew a breath up at the hair tumbling in her eyes. She turned back toward the truck and his heart squeezed. He'd blown it. Somewhere in that muddied, dumbass explanation he'd shot his chance to hell. But instead of getting in the truck, she tossed her purse inside and pivoted to race across the six feet separating them.

He braced, catching her as she slammed into him. Her legs wrapped around his hips, her arms around his neck and then she kissed him. He devoured her mouth, meeting her eager tongue with his own. She was soft and curvy beneath the dress. His hands closed over her bottom, kneading it through the material. She'd always been soft.

But her girlish figure was beautifully rounded now. In the hind part of his brain, he recognized she'd put on weight, but it filled out all the right parts of her body. The woman in his arms was like a live grenade and his body was the clip. Her mouth moved to his jaw and when her teeth bit down on his throat, he laughed. Her greedy little mouth always left hickeys.

God, I hope she leaves one right now.

"Make love to me, Luke." The words lodged next to his heart, shoving away the last barricade to the past.

"It's a thirty minute drive to the house," he groaned. His cock was so hard, he regretted the fit of his dress pants. "But I think we can make it in fifteen."

"No." She leaned back, trusting her weight to his hands, her fingers playing with the short hairs at the nape of his neck. He needed a haircut.

And a shave.

And a shower.

And some roses.

Hell, he needed a *lot* of roses.

Wait, did she just say no?

"Babe?" The word came out on a harsh exhale.

"No. No driving, no house, no waiting. Right now. Right there." She jerked her thumb toward the truck. "You have a blanket in the back seat."

His body revved at the thought. "But sweetheart, it's *cold*."

"So, you don't think you can warm me up, Marine?" Her lips twitched into a saucy smile and rusty laughter wheezed out of him. Yeah, he could warm her up. He strode toward the truck, every step bumping her hips with his, teasing the hell out of him. He would die if he didn't get her clothes off.

She started to slide down and he squeezed her ass, pressing her against him. His cock swelled further. "Uh uh. No moving, missy. I got this."

Her mouth closed on his earlobe and pleasure zinged through him. He one armed open the back door, grabbed his go pack and tossed the whole lot into the bed of the truck. Two rolled blankets followed.

"You came prepared." Silky amusement colored the voice whispering in his ear and Luke shoved the door shut and carried her around to the back. One click and the gate opened. A hard look around the area revealed they were very much alone and no cameras pointed at the truck. Satisfied, he hoisted her up and followed, barely letting her slide away as she scooched to grab the blankets.

They tripped over each other, laughing as they spread the blankets out. Her fingers went back to the buttons on his shirt and he searched for whatever the hell held her dress together. "Strip, Marine." The amused arousal thickened her voice.

"Yes ma'am."

She inched back, peeling out of her dress and his tongue had to be hanging out as the dress vanished, leaving only creamy pale skin, full breasts and hard nipples peeking over the top of two scraps of lace she'd tied together to make a bra. Her pantyhose came next and joined his shirt, belt and pants. His shoes and socks were an afterthought, but he could only stare at the long length of her tanned legs and the scraps of pale skin around her barely-there panties.

"You are so damn beautiful." And she was. He had to slow down before he embarrassed himself and came inside his shorts.

"Stop talking, Marine. The action's right here." The teasing quirk to the corner of her mouth, the spark in her eyes—this was his Rebecca. All fiery passion, spitfire and love.

So much damn love.

"Are you sure? I know I made a mess of that apology and you have every right to...."

She surged up from the blanket, meeting him breast to chest, her fingers covering his mouth. "Shh...it's always been you. Always. I never wanted anyone else. I thought I got past it, I was over it and I was moving on. But every guy who ever asked me out, I measured against you and they all came up short. I. Love. You." She punctuated the last three words with a kiss, her cool fingers stroking over his chest.

He knew the moment she found the scars. A burn from a fight in Kandahar. A cluster of three puckered scars from bullets in Kabul. A thick slash from shrapnel in a city he couldn't remember. Her gaze shifted down and her lips trailed down his jaw to his chest. She stroked each scar gently, before laving her tongue over them. Each touch of her lips added balm to the deeper scars, the ones stretching into his soul.

"We wasted so much time. Please don't make me wait anymore, Luke."

He groaned. He could deny her nothing. He tugged her upward, catching her mouth with his. He bit down on her lower lip and shifted her until she lay down against the rough blanket. He barely noticed the scratchy and durable fabric as he took his own time kissing down to her chest. Her bra unhooked in the front, a thought he was vaguely glad for or he would have just ripped it off.

Her sharp cry when his lips rasped over one turgid nipple filled him with satisfaction. He teased it with his teeth, tugging until her fingers closed on his head, before moving to the other and showering it with the same attention. Goose pimples rippled over her flesh, and he blew against the second damp nipple.

He could dine there for hours, playing with her breasts, and feasting on her responses. His fingers slid down to the thin scrap of black. He tugged it, tearing the barely-there panties wide open to explore the damp curls. His cock jerked at the silken heat waiting between her nether lips.

"You're so wet," he whispered, half in wonder, half in pleasure-drunken stupor. He stroked the lips apart, teasing the hard, throbbing nub pulsing beneath his thumb. Her moans grew louder and she cried out, spasming against his fingers. He tilted his gaze upward, watching her mouth open and close as he continued to tease her sex. Her orgasm drenched his fingers and he stroked her through it.

Pure, masculine satisfaction rolled through him. He wanted to taste that orgasm and he scooted downwards, his mouth trailing wet kisses across her trembling belly to the curls. The scent of her filled his nostrils. She was so feminine. He tasted sweet vanilla and musky female.

"Luke!" His name bolted from her lips as he stroked his tongue down the wet cleft, lapping at the cream waiting for him. He nosed her clit, intent on being drunk on the scent of her. How many licks to the center of her orgasm drifted across his mind, and he slid his hands under her bottom, lifting her into a better position.

Fingers stroking her anus, he locked his lips around her sweet clit and sucked. She shuddered. Thrumming his tongue against the swollen nub, he laughed as her body twisted, buttocks tightening and the hard catch to her voice warned him that another orgasm approached. Lapping harder, he drove her on. His balls ached when she came. The sweet cream of her orgasm flooded his mouth and he drank her up, his finger pressing into her anus even as her hips bucked up to him.

"Luke." Her voice stretched out in a hoarse, tortured whisper. He petted her through the orgasm, sliding his finger gently in and out as his tongue mirrored the motion against her sex. He wanted to begin there every night for the rest of her life. He would go to sleep drunk on the taste of her. Her fingers pulled at his shoulders, her nails scraping his skin urgent.

"...you...I need you...."

"I'm coming, baby." He comforted her, one last stroke of his tongue for luck across her drenched sex before sliding up her body. Her hands tugged at his boxers, shoving them down. He paused at her breasts, worshipping each nipple before kicking the boxers into the darkness. The cool air only increased the heat burning between them. His cock bobbed with eagerness as he shifted, grabbing a condom from his discarded pants pockets. Sheathed, he knelt between her legs, his body aching as the tip of his cock brushed against her wet entrance.

He reached between them, his gaze watching her face. He wanted to watch every nuance of her expression as he sank into her. Her hand wrapped around the head of his cock, her thumb stroking the moisture from the slit and then she guided him, pressing him against her entrance, hips lifting to pull him in when he sank home.

Heat locked around him. She was tight. *So gloriously tight.*

One thrust and the last barrier between them fell.

His insides jerked and his eyes widened.

She's a virgin.

"Don't you dare." She wrapped her legs around him, pulling him deeper, taking every, hard inch of him.

His balls were going to explode.

"Rebecca," he groaned, diving in for a kiss.

"Love me, Luke. Just love me."

Always.

He sank into her, holding on to sanity by his fingertips while she got used to him. He wasn't a small man and she was so damn, deliciously tight. But her impatient nails raked along his ass and up his back and then he thrust again, driving into her slowly at first, but with increased tempo.

He wanted her pleasure to last forever, but even as he tried to slow down, her hips rose up to meet him greedily stealing the pace away. His balls slapped against her ass and then he came, hard, violent jets of pleasure that turned his insides to jelly. He shook with release and imagined filling her to the brim, marking every sweet part of her sex with the scent of him.

Mine.

She's always been mine.

She always will be.

Collapsing, he took care not to crush her, but she refused to unwind from him and let him roll away. Sweet kisses touched his face, brushed along his cheek and teased his mouth.

"So." Her voice blew out on a breathy whisper. "What are we doing tomorrow night?"

Laughter wheezed out of him. Rising up on his arms, he gazed down at her sweat-dampened face. Grabbing the second blanket, he pulled it over them, trapping their body heat lest she begin shivering. "Why didn't you tell me?"

"What? That I'm a twenty-eight-year-old virgin?" Shyness drifted across her face and she ducked her chin.

"Hey." Luke nuzzled her cheek, gently nudging her expression away from the shadows. "It's okay."

"No it's not," she laughed, shifting beneath him to rub her face with one hand. "I always wanted you. I had this idea in my head that after playoffs and divisionals that year, it would be you and me and we could explore it. But then you left and I just...I never wanted anyone else."

"Ever, baby?" He frowned, torn between delight and discomfort.

"Nope. I told you I compared every other man to you and the older I got, the easier it was just to ignore it. They weren't you."

"So why were you in the bar tonight?" Curiosity stretched in him, claws threatening to puncture the perfect moment. But he wanted to know. He wanted to know everything, every thought, every dream, every nuance of her expression. He had ten years of catching up to do and he wanted to start right then.

"Promise you won't laugh?" Her cheeks pinkened, the flush spreading up from her neck and setting her eyes sparkling. His sweet Rebecca remained the innocent, cheerful girl wrapped in a woman's body.

"I give you my word." He'd have sworn anything. His fingers drifted up to stroke the tendrils of hair away from her face, balancing his weight on his elbows so that he could keep her warm, but not crush her.

"My business partner bullied me into signing up for this dating service...."

"...1Night Stand." Luke finished the thought for her, amused.

"Yes, how did you—no—really?" Her shyness evaporated on the wings of her own amusement. Her laughter vibrated through him as her inner walls contracted around him.

I'm gonna need a new condom in a minute.

Several, in fact.

And a bed.

"Yes, guilty as charged, ma'am. Guilty as charged."

"Why did you sign up for a dating service?"

"For the unit. Some of the guys, they just don't know how to connect with people, new people, anymore. It can be hard, to date, to meet women, to risk putting themselves out there. We made a pact. We all signed up, we all got vetted."

"No *I* in team," she whispered, lifting her hand to run it over his jaw.

He tilted his head to catch her passing fingers in a kiss. "No ma'am. There is no *I* in team. But there is one right here and he's all for you. I know one night doesn't change everything, but...."

"It's a start, Luke. I never stopped loving you."

"I love you, too." Damn, but the words sounded great in his head, his heart and his soul. If she weren't naked, he'd stand up in the bed of the truck and shout it to the world.

"So, you never answered my question earlier." She stroked her fingers through his hair, her nails teasing his scalp, the gesture both soothing and erotic.

"What was your question, sweetheart?" He'd give her whatever she wanted, whenever she wanted it. They had a lot of time to make up.

"What are we doing tomorrow night?"

Tell it to the Marine

Heather Long

&

Chapter One

*J*ames Westwood leaned back in the chair, one ankle resting on the opposite knee. Matt McCall paced the far wall of his office, shaking with restless energy. Most of their sessions began with Matt sitting, but he always bounced to his feet and started pacing within thirty minutes. By the fifty-minute mark, he looked for escape.

"Have you been practicing the breathing exercises?" James wanted to draw him back to the session. Laid out with heavy furniture, comfortable chairs, and a tinted picture window, his office overlooked a sunken garden populated by flowers, shrubbery, tall trees, and an artificial spring. The soothing symmetry seemed to be having little effect on Matt.

At the end of the sofa, Matt paused and braced his hands against the frame, fingers digging into it. His lips were white with tension.

"Yes, I've been trying. They work, sometimes. Other times, I just can't sit still. I can't *not* pace. I went for a run last night. Couldn't seem to stop."

"How far did you make it?"

"Twelve miles."

James wrote that down on his white pad and offered the man a small smile. "That's better than last week. You went fifteen."

"My mom called." Just twenty-four, Matt had served overseas for five years following his basic training. He'd still be with his unit if not for the death of his father coming hot on the heels of the crash he and several of his men suffered in a helicopter accident. The damage to his inner ear had left him with partial deafness and equilibrium issues.

"How is Margaret?" The catalyst for Matt's tension seemed directly related to his inability to reconnect with his family, his friends, and his life beyond the Marines. *I should give Logan a call. He should be back from Las Vegas. He might get more out of Matt in a pick-up game.*

"She's mom." Matt shrugged. "She wants me to make plans to come home for the holidays. They're months away, but with Dad gone, she wants me to swear that I'll be there, and I don't...."

His fists clenched and he pounded them on the sofa, before bowing his head and sucking in a noisy breath. A vein in his forehead throbbed, the skin flushing around his high and tight haircut.

"Why the hell is this so hard?" He lifted blazing blue eyes and glared across the room. "We've been talking for weeks and it's not better. I still can't sleep. I still can't focus. Captain Dexter said you could help me, so why the hell do I want to curl into a ball and cry like a child after I talk to my mother? She needs me."

James let the anger roll off him like water off a duck's back. "It takes time, Matt. Time to acclimate. Time to identify your triggers. Time to develop new habits. Did you write down the moment the call went badly?"

"Yeah." The Marine flung himself down on the sofa, knuckles white from clenching his fists. "She said the kids need me there. Dad's gone and the pool needs fixing, the fence is worn, and one of the toilets broke upstairs."

James flicked a look at the clock. They had five minutes left on the session. Not enough time. Anything past fifty minutes could leave his patient too emotionally drained. "Did she say she wanted you to fix them or was she just filling you in on what was going on?" His kept his tone neutral, easy.

Matt paused and shook his head. "I don't know. We were talking about me, then we talked about some party Lizzie is going to. Lizzie's sixteen and Mom wanted to know if I remembered some of her friends. She worried that a couple are messing around with shit they shouldn't be into. Then she started talking about problems with a repairman...." He trailed off, scrubbing a hand around the back of his neck. "I asked her what repairman?"

"And she told you what needed fixing."

Matt slumped back, his expression pensive. "Yeah."

"When did the holiday talk come up?"

"At the beginning...she's trying to plan ahead for food."

James waited.

"Hell, they didn't have anything to do with each other."

A breakthrough and their time was up. For once, they ended the session with Matt sitting instead of wearing a hole through the plush carpet Mike's Place had installed in James' office.

"Good stuff today, Matt. Keep journaling. Yes, it's sissy crap, but it's an order." James spared him a smile. "I'm off site tonight. Ken will be here. But if you're up for it, maybe we can run tomorrow."

He liked to run to stay in shape and some of his patients felt more comfortable talking to him on the move. He stood and offered his hand to Matt, glad for the man's quick shake.

"Thanks, sir." Matt bounced to his feet and out the door in thirty seconds, jettisoning the office like a submarine releasing its ballast for an emergency surfacing. James carried his white legal pad over to the desk and flipped through Matt's folder. *PFC Matt McCall honorably discharged due to permanent medical disability.* He'd come to Mike's Place after meeting James at the funeral for Matt's father. A funeral he attended at the private request of the chaplain for Matt's unit. She worried about him.

James worried about him, too.

The cell phone in his desk drawer hummed. He pulled the drawer open and read the message with a half smile.

Sybarite Club. 7 PM. Blonde woman, 5'9, will wear a yellow rose necklace. Her name is Lauren and she prefers white wine to red.

He paused, studying the message. Lauren. Gorgeous name.

The basic description lacked any real visual. Another glance at his watch showed five after four. He had to type up his notes, shower, and change if he wanted to make it to the Sybarite Club in downtown Dallas on time.

CB

Two hours later, he jogged down the path to the parking lot. He loved the layout of Mike's Place. It was as much a community park as sports complex with private apartments for permanent residents and guest villas for visiting families. Its layout offered wide open spaces, with plenty of room for running or, as some residents were doing, flopping in the grass for quiet reading time. The builders framed most of the complex around the heavy trees indigenous to the area, keeping it shady even in Texas' simmering one hundred-degree summers.

September brought little relief from the heat of summer—in fact, it brought only about ten degrees of relief to the sultry ninety degrees without the promise of rain.

"Hey, Doc!" Logan Cavanaugh jogged toward him from the opposite direction. His sweat pants and loose black T-shirt, too dark for the autumn heat, were soaked through. The left corner of his mouth permanently turned down in a grimace by the scar tissue that spread from his cheek to his throat and below, a reminder of the burning, twisted metal coffin he'd survived and the five surgeries that included three pins, one in his knee, one his hip and the last one in the shoulder.

"Hey. Just the man I planned to call tomorrow. How did it go in Vegas?"

Logan and his best friend Zach had taken a long weekend in Vegas as part of a 1Night Stand date. The dark cloud that often surged around the Marine seemed absent.

"Pretty damn good." Logan grinned. "Hell...better than good."

"Excellent." While Logan wasn't a regular patient, they'd struck up camaraderie during Logan's early rehabilitation.

"Yeah, well, you know that little problem I had? All gone." The

Marine grinned wider and gave him a thumbs up.

James laughed. "Congratulations."

"Thank you. Thank you very much. So, what did you need?" Instead of standing, Logan continued to jog in place, keeping his muscles warm. He couldn't run flat out anymore, but months of therapy allowed him more mobility than the doctors hoped for. He'd obviously embraced his latest therapy of jogging.

"You know Matt McCall?" A long shot. Just because they were Marines didn't mean they knew each other. In fact, with so many new arrivals over the last three months, there were a number of unfamiliar faces working toward a new life at Mike's Place.

Logan shook his head. "Can't say that I do."

"Well if you have time tomorrow, maybe you could join us for a run or a pick-up."

"Three on three?"

"Sounds like a plan."

"Zach's got some kids running scrimmages in the morning, but after that I'm free. Just text me. I'll be here."

"Will do."

"Have a good time on your date tonight...."

He paused. "Who said I had a date?"

"Shiny shoes, fresh shave, thousand dollar suit. Says it all." Logan winked and jogged on.

James laughed and twirled his keys around his forefinger. Zach's plan to bring Logan back to life with a threesome seemed to have been successful. It wasn't his idea of a good time, but one could not argue with results.

An hour later, at five minutes to seven, he handed his keys off to a valet driver. A red square corset framed her generous breasts perfectly and a filmy white shirt opened to show the cleavage. Tugging his wallet out, he traded the valet slip for the plain black card with the silver lettering. Dallas' Sybarite Club offered every pleasure from music to food to companionship and private rooms. Unlike some exclusive clubs, it catered to men and women alike as long as they presented an all-access pass.

The doorman—a tall, lanky figure dressed in a topcoat and

tails who seemed to have stepped right out of the roaring twenties—accepted the card and scanned it with a small palm device. The technology wasn't in keeping with the man's old world atmosphere, but he returned the card with a pleasant smile.

"Welcome to the Sybarite Club, Mr. Westwood. Your dining companion arrived ten minutes ago." He motioned toward gothic-style doors carved from dark cherry and decorated with woodcuts of a man and woman engaged in cunnilingus and fellatio. As the doors parted, each figure seemed to cry out. James wasn't sure if their silent mouths were opened in pleasure or frustration.

The carpeted entryway descended four steps into a lounge with a dark, almost jazzy pseudo-gothic atmosphere. Flickering candles complemented the low lighting. Long shadows twisted across the textured booths, bar stools, and tables. Three couples swayed together on the dance floor to the smooth sounds of blues. Instruments on the empty stage suggested a potential for live music.

He'd heard a lot about the Sybarite Club but never had the occasion to visit the establishment. Surveying the room, he noted the servers in black outfits slipping in and out of the lounge, ghosts who didn't disturb the guests except to take orders or deliver them. Three tables held couples or threesomes chatting over drinks. A fourth held only empty chairs.

Probably one of the dancing couples.

The booths were tucked into the wall making it harder to see who sat there.

"Mr. Westwood?" A slim waitress smiled up at him, a tray tucked between her arm and torso.

"Yes?"

"Your party is this way, sir." She beckoned him down the red-carpeted steps into the lounge proper, and he followed her path through the club to a tall-backed booth in the back. Still acclimating to the low lighting, he couldn't make out the occupant save for the slender feminine arm reaching for her wine glass on the table.

A curl of excitement twisted in his gut. He'd planned to keep the date low key, but the club, the music, and the atmosphere teased his anticipation. The waitress halted with a sweep of her arm to allow him to precede her.

"Can I get you anything, Mr. Westwood?"

"Soda water with lime, please." He preferred to keep his wits about him. "And bottle of whatever the lady is having." If they were going to have a dinner, he could do at least provide her with her preferred wine.

"Of course."

Free of the waitress' distraction he turned back to the booth. A golden-haired goddess stared up at him. Sea-blue eyes seemed to catch every drop of light in the room and reflect it in shimmering azure. She rose to offer him her hand and his heart hesitated a beat.

"James?" Milk and honey flowed through her voice and his spine straightened, his cock already jerking into a salute. "I'm...."

"Lauren Kincaid." He could only hope he wasn't drooling like a lovesick fool. *Lauren Kincaid, movie goddess, is my one-night stand?*

Her candid laughter, low and throaty, tingled against his ears and he grinned. Shaking off his shock, he took her extended hand and shook it carefully. His larger hand totally engulfed her slender fingers, and he didn't want to squeeze her with excitement.

"It's a pleasure to meet you." Her charming smile flashed with warmth that rolled over him from head to toe.

"Ma'am, you have no idea." His date was Lauren Kincaid. The only chick flick star he would pay money to see. With or without a date.

Chapter Two

*S*he rose with practiced grace. Years of performing in front of a camera with only a thirty-minute nap and a cup of decaf to stave off exhaustion had made her a master of poise and controlled expression. A talent she was immensely grateful for because she'd glanced out of the booth to see the tall, athletic man with his broad shoulders, tan skin, and sexy-as-sin smile a full sixty seconds before the waitress led him to her booth.

She barely managed to sit back and reach for her wine glass to steady her nerves and back-flipping stomach. If one could blend Hugh Jackman's engaging smile and Dwayne Johnson's broad shoulders with Chris Hemsworth's physique, they would have created James. The description she'd received via text promised a six-foot four dining companion with sandy blond hair, a dimpled cheek and a passion for long conversations about "life, the universe and everything." The Douglas Adams quote was enough to soothe her unease over a blind one-night stand.

"It's a pleasure to meet you." And it was. Ironic considering she'd turned around twice on her way to the date, both times having to consciously recite the three reasons she'd allowed her agent to sign her up for the mysterious Madame Eve's 1Night Stand. She wanted a night with a real man, with no vested interest in how she could help his career. She wanted to explore genuine options, to descend from the glass walls of exposure where being seen was what it was all about. And, she wanted a night that was just about her and the delicious man standing in front of her.

As they shook hands, she couldn't help the smile pulling her mouth wide. She didn't need to pretend pleasure at meeting him or the simple delight at the emotion rippling across his expression lighting up his slate gray eyes.

"Ma'am, you have no idea." The cultured gentleman with the air of small town charm continued to hold her hand.

"Well, perhaps you can enlighten me." Her knees quivered and she was glad she'd chosen the pale champagne silk dress with its bodice cupping top and floor length skirt. James released her with a hint of reluctance and gestured toward the booth.

Barely managing to contain the wild butterflies rioting in her belly, she swept a smoothing hand across her hip before sitting. Fortunately pure silk didn't wrinkle, so sitting wouldn't leave a crinkled line across her ass.

Thank God I worked out this morning.

He waited a beat until she'd settled before sliding in across from her. She was at once irritated and delighted by their private booth. Delighted for the intimacy of the small table and the privacy it afforded and irritated that he was far away, around the curve of the booth to sit opposite her.

Slow down. We can afford to take a moment and absorb. He hasn't said much and the gorgeous packaging is just window dressing. Her libido wasn't remotely interested in the practical thoughts. She crossed one leg over the other, foot bumping his long legs under the table. A quiver of heat shivered in her belly.

"I have a confession to make." Her first rule of dating shattered without a backward glance. She never started the conversation. After ten years of boring dates with men who only seemed to know how to talk about themselves, she'd learned the best barometer of her interest was to let her date take the lead. She could tell in five minutes or less whether dinner would make it to dessert or drinks afterward and within another ten whether they would be saying goodnight at the restaurant.

"Oh?" He shifted in the seat, the warmth of his leg stretching away from hers a fraction, allowing her crossed legs space but still close enough that she regretted insisting on a public meeting location.

"Yes." Wrapping her fingers around the wine glass for courage, she tried to edge aside the schoolgirl jitters to meet his even look. "I've never decided to have sex with a man after one glance before."

His mouth opened, a hint of shock flattening his dimples.

Way to play that subtle, Kincaid. Where did you learn your technique? The Bachelor?

"Thank you, I think. And I'll see your confession with one of my own. I *have* decided that I would have sex with a woman at one glance before."

Straightforward, blunt-edged honesty without arrogance. *Where the hell has this guy been hiding?*

"Oh?" She played with fire.

The waitress returned with a chilled bottle of wine in an ice bucket for her and a square, tumbled glass with ice and a splash of something clear and bubbly for him. "Would you care to hear the specials tonight?"

He glanced at Lauren, eyebrows raised in inquiry. Smile widening, she nodded a silent assent. "Please," he told the waitress. She listed off several dishes, but Lauren barely heard her. He canted his head to the side, his expression attentive and patient throughout the full list.

"What would you like?" The smoky, sex-on-a-stick gray gaze slid toward her and she had to fight the urge to bite her lip.

"The parmesan encrusted salmon, fresh vegetables and lemon spears, white rice." He was steak medium rare, and baked potato with butter and sour cream, and avocado bread.

He's chocolate-drizzled cheesecake and white chocolate dipped strawberries, too. Stop drooling.

The waitress smiled and disappeared with their order. Dabbing her mouth with the napkin, Lauren took a drink of wine to buy her composure some time. "So, how did that go?"

"How did what go, ma'am?"

"The woman you wanted to have sex with at one glance."

"I don't know. We just met." It could have been a line, but the simplicity and directness coupled in his tone melted her reservations.

"Well, you will definitely have to let me know how that turns out." She raised her wine glass.

"You will be the first to know." He clinked his tumbler to her glass and grinned.

"So what do you do, James with no last name?"

He set down his drink and frowned. "I apologize. James Westwood, ma'am."

"It's a pleasure, James Westwood, and please, call me Lauren, not ma'am."

"Yes, ma—Lauren."

They both laughed, the artificial tension melting like the ice in his glass.

"I'm a psychologist, boring on the surface, I suppose. But a field I enjoy."

"It doesn't sound boring, I played a psychologist once." *Lame, Lauren. Lame. "Look you do something real for a living, but I played one on TV."* She swallowed another mouthful of wine to cover her discomfort.

"You were charming. I loved watching you trying to ferret out the murderer." He turned his glass in an easy circle on its napkin.

"Yes, well, I wouldn't have sent patients to me. I barely understood the issue the profilers were describing or why my character was so defensive." *And can we stop talking about my career...isn't that what bores the hell out of me when every other date I've had does it?*

"I don't know. You disagreed on the underlying cause, and as it turns out you were right. The triggers were not psychosexual and indirect, but directly related to his immature understanding of social interactions due to a lifetime of bullying. The man literally couldn't comprehend kindness, which was why the perp kept coming back to see your character week in and week out. You were the first one to accept him for who he was and why, when he experienced the break, he didn't hurt her and she was able to talk him down."

"Well, when you put it that way...I was brilliant."

He laughed, a kind, cheerful sound devoid of any condescension or judgment and she grinned.

"Half of my job is listening, hearing what a patient says. Too often we don't really listen to the people around us. We talk to them, we listen to them talk, but we don't hear them. We judge people whether it's a social situation or business relationship, we categorize the worth and value of their words before they even open their mouth. In some cases, we label them and box them up as people and never allow them to step beyond those parameters because we don't want to hear it."

The waitress returned with a pair of walnut apple salads sprinkled with feta cheese, then quickly and efficiently left them to their privacy.

"How can we not want to hear the people we care about?" Lauren picked up her fork and speared an apple slice. "Doesn't the act of conversation suggest that we want to hear what someone else is saying?"

"Yes and no. When we talk, we want the person we are speaking to, to hear us and share our emotions with regard to the topic of conversation. Case in point, you wanted to relate to my profession so you mentioned what you played on television. It's not the same thing and you were a bit embarrassed about it, but...." He waved his fork at her when she opened her mouth, the already mentioned embarrassment creeping up to warm her cheeks. "But it also demonstrated that you were trying to empathize with me. You did hear me and you wanted to create a common space for our conversation."

"And here I thought it a little vain and pretentious by asking you to pay attention to my career, and I hate bringing up my career." *Thank God for dim lighting. I must be beet red at this point.*

"But you're an actress—it's what you do. Why would it be vain or pretentious to bring up your body of work?"

She crunched the apple thoughtfully, considering her answer. "Because...it's lame? I have people who come up to me all the time, acting like they really know me or really love me because they saw me in some movie or some program and it gives them the right to this intimate acquaintance with me. I deal with actors and their egos all the time...."

Why is it always so hard to put my thoughts into actual words? Do I really need a script for this?

"At the risk of sounding clinical, you have every right to refer to your career and your experiences for the purposes of conversation and worry about the awkwardness that I might be interested in you only for those experiences." He chewed a mouthful of salad, gaze never wavering. "For the record, you stole my breath away in *Once Smitten, Twice Shy*, but any intimacy I want to experience, I want to do so with the woman across the table from me, not the lady on the screen."

"You're direct."

"Best way to avoid miscommunication is to say what you mean. Mean what you say." The wry hint of self-deprecation didn't escape her.

"You didn't sound clinical...okay, maybe a little...but I like that you seem to understand my babble."

"It's not babble. It's conversation. We can talk about your work. We can *not* talk about your work. You can finish that salad and dance with me. Or we can talk about the Cowboys...."

"That's a sports team, right?" She hid a smile behind another bite of salad, the sweet tart of the apple enhanced by the smooth, smoky feta and lemony lettuce.

"I know. You're a Raiders girl."

"Actually, I'm more of a Lakers girl. I look fabulous on those big screens sitting courtside." She grinned when he laughed again. She loved the deep, throaty quality of his laugh without any hint of nasal distraction or worse, the polite tee hee of humoring the blonde.

"Been to any games recently? A lot of the guys recorded them. I can check it out for myself."

"During the playoffs. My agent wanted me to make nice with the lead in the movie I auditioned for—you know, see and be seen, get some buzz on TMZ—and see if the casting director went for it." The tabloids loved her ringside positioning next to the Hollywood bad boy with his oversexed reputation and permanent bachelor status.

She hated that part of her job. The auditions were professional, but all the 'play for the press' made her look like an exhibitionist. Lately, a desperate exhibitionist trying to cling to her youth.

"Did you get the part?" A guarded look came over his expression.

"Nope. I'm actually kind of glad because the man didn't seem to understand the need for Tic Tacs before you whisper in someone's face. He smelled like hot dogs and bad coffee."

The waitress reappeared, stealing away their salads and setting their meals in front of them.

"Good. Well, not good," He frowned dropping his gaze to his plate. Her heart bounced like a puppy scrabbling for attention. "Sorry, would you like more wine?"

"Yes, please. And why are you sorry?" She slid her wine glass toward him, and he refilled it carefully.

"Being happy you didn't get a job doesn't seem like the right thing."

"It depends on why you were happy. Because if you knew about the production, then you might be happy that I'm not somewhere in Indiana filming right now. Or you could be happy because the lead has a lecherous reputation and has slept with every woman he's ever shared screen time with. Or you could simply be happy that I didn't want to kiss him...." She lifted the wine glass to her lips, daring him with a playful look.

"Fine. I'm not sorry at all that you didn't get the part because I'm extremely happy you're not in Indiana, nor being pawed by a letch whose arms would need to be broken, and that you didn't want to kiss him."

Her sex clenched. "I'm glad I didn't get the part, too."

"Are you glad because you didn't want to kiss him? Because you didn't want to sleep with him? Or because you wouldn't be at dinner with me?"

An hour ago, she wanted to be anywhere but the Sybarite Club waiting for some stranger with expectations of sex no matter how libidinous her needs were. An hour ago she'd argued with her agent on the phone about the latest offer to play mom to Aqua Williams, Hollywood's latest *It* girl in a role that she herself would have been offered ten years before.

An hour ago, she hadn't met James Westwood and decided that kissing him would be better than cheesecake dipped in melted chocolate or that lead in the next action film would be poor recompense for the laughter-tinged desire humming through her system.

"Lauren?"

"Hmm?" She covered her mouth mid-chew and swallowed the salmon with a choked chuckle. "Sorry, I think that I was happy I didn't get the part because I wouldn't have known what I missed, meeting you. I really thought this whole thing was a bad idea...."

"Which segues beautifully into the question I wanted to ask, but didn't want to offend you." He set his knife down and captured her hand. Her insides somersaulted. His calloused thumb stroked her palm.

"I'll show you mine if you show me yours." She shattered her second rule of dating. Although hardly *fait accompli*, she didn't care if he'd signed up because he just wanted to get laid. She hadn't had so much fun in a long time.

He slid out of the booth, still holding her hand. "Dance with me."

She let him tug her out of the booth. "I can't dance."

"Fine. Step on my toes with me."

Curiosity trumped nerves and she nodded, following him onto the dance floor and gliding into his arms, barely aware of the drifting melody of sobbing saxophone and nerve-thumping guitar. Up close, cradled against the warmth of his chest, enjoying the beat of his heart against his ribs beneath her palm, she found her four-inch heels gave her no advantage to his height. The cage of his body wrapped around hers, pulling her into a gentle to and fro sway far sexier and simpler than any choreographed number she'd had to practice.

"Why a one-night stand, Lauren?"

"You'll think it's stupid."

"Let me be the judge of that." He leaned in, his forehead just millimeters from hers, the sweet hints of Old Spice, cotton, and something deeply masculine filled her lungs.

"Because I spend all my time playing to egos, catering to what the audience wants, and meeting men who play the same parts...I wanted to meet someone real. Not an actor with an agenda or a director with plan...but a real, honest-to-God man with no other agenda beyond an entertaining evening."

She bit her lip, forcing her gaze up to meet his bold directness. "I wanted a night of simple pleasures, man, woman, food...and if sex happened, I wanted it to be spectacular and all about mutual pleasure...not for career advancement or some egotistic need to punch a notch on a belt."

"I promise." His voice melted over her. "If sex happens, it will definitely be all about mutual pleasure."

Chapter Three

*S*he flowed beautifully in his arms, satin, silk, and softness drifting to the music. He fought to keep his hands from roaming. Her blue eyes watched him from beneath the thick fringe of her lashes. The artless smiles, the raw honesty, and the flicker of nervous ticks in her hand gestures bulldozed every reservation he'd had about the date. From the first email he'd received from the mysterious Madame Eve to the moment he'd walked up to the table, his plan remained simple: enjoy a meal, some quiet conversation, and say good night.

Yes, he'd signed up for the 1Night Stand along with every other man in the unit. A show of solidarity for their brothers who needed the opportunity to meet someone, to reintegrate with the big bad world far away from the fierce and fast rules of the sandbox. But meeting her changed everything.

"Your turn, James." Her voice possessed a husky quality that slid through his system like a well-aged whisky, heating every nerve it touched. "Why did you sign up?"

True to her word, her foot stepped on his, but he ignored the pinch of her shoe and the scrape across the top of his loafers. She couldn't weigh more than a hundred pounds soaking wet. He could polish out the scuffmarks later.

"I spent a few years in the sandbox, received an honorable discharge, came home and finished my degree. The day I received my certification and license, I had a call from Captain Dexter. I'd reported to him during my first tour. Good man. He opened a facility here in Allen called Mike's Place. Heard of it?"

She shook her head and the waterfall of champagne blonde hair danced in a caress against her shoulders. A cluster of strawberries shadowed her right shoulder, a birthmark he didn't recall seeing on the screen. Hand skimming up her arm, he drew a thumb across the mark. An unfamiliar tug pulled behind his sternum. Cataloging differences between the smoking hot sweetheart on the big screen and the exquisite femininity in his arms was a hobby he could embrace.

"It's a facility predicated on helping our brothers. It begins with therapy, physical, mental, and emotional. It offers rehabilitation for physical injuries, post-operative recovery support, group and individual therapy. We have a hospital wing for patients who need more intensive care and an outpatient wing for locals and those who live in the guest residences."

"It sounds very well thought out."

"It's brilliant, actually. The Captain—Luke—is a dedicated Marine. He puts his men first. He added guest residences for out-of-state patients and their families, and apartments for staff. There's a sports complex, a daycare and in the next six months, a full-time charter school with our own instructors for children of staff and patients. We don't just focus on our brothers, but offer support for the whole family. Luke's planning to expand over the next year to include care for widowed spouses and their children."

The music shifted to a slower tempo and he paused to tug her closer until her body rested breast to chest with his and her thighs gently glided against his in a rasp of fabric.

"And you work there?" She murmured the words.

"Yes, I focused my thesis and clinical on trauma support. Reintegration after the sandbox is difficult in the best of circumstances, but when you combine physical injury or personal loss, you raise the emotional stakes, and we're wired for combat, not civilian life. It takes time to reacclimatize."

Her perfume carried hints of flowers and candy, like a breeze blowing from a bakery shop on a spring day. His cock jerked hopefully and he focused on a stand-down order. He wanted to take his time and savor every moment.

"You must have an amazing soul."

Pleasure spiked at the compliment, but his brows quirked. "How so, ma—Lauren?" He'd get that right, sooner or later.

She laughed, but didn't comment on his near slip. "Because I can't imagine how hard it must be for you. You served there and you have to relive that to help others."

"They're my brothers, nothing I wouldn't do for them."

"And who helped you when you came home?" The insightful question cut through the layers of separation, dividing James the man from James the psychologist.

"My work helps me every day. I knew the minute I received my discharge orders what I wanted to do. How I could help them. If I couldn't be over there to cover their backs, I could damn well cover them here. Pardon my language."

"You are forgiven."

He turned them along the edge of the dance floor, drifting to the bluesy number. Her hands glided up his arms until her fingers interlocked behind his neck. The action lifted her breasts, cupped beautifully by the dress, and he allowed one look, searing it in his brain before retreating to stare into her eyes. Not that much of a retreat. The warm softness of her curves still pressed into him, and it didn't take much of a leap to imagine riding between her bare thighs, her legs wrapped around his hips.

One battle at a time, Marine.

"You still haven't answered my question. I don't think." Her forehead crinkled in a thoughtful frown.

"No, you're correct. I just wanted you to have a firm basis for understanding my decision. Madame Eve offers an unparalleled service that seems to pair ideal couples together for meaningful interactions that may or may not lead to sex." He tacked on the last as a reminder to his engorged cock, but the organ ignored him, wholly focused on the goddess in his arms.

"For some of our guys, it's been the perfect way to meet someone with no strings, no expectations but still allow meaningful experience, plugging them back into the world, building confidence. That's especially important because intimacy can't be forced. The Marines who truly need it were reluctant to sign up until Luke volunteered all of us."

The music drifted to a lonely, final note that hung in the air and they slowed. She took one step back. Instead of withdrawing, she ran a hand down his arm and threaded her fingers through his. James took the cue and led her back to the table. Rather than reclaim her seat, she chose his side of the booth and scooted until he could slide in next to her.

He took a moment to push her dinner plate toward her, along with a fresh glass of wine.

"That's really beautiful, you know? And so much more classy than my reasons." Her pink-tinged lips twisted into a self-deprecating smile.

"Not at all. There isn't anything I wouldn't do for my brothers, but—and I mean this with absolute sincerity—signing up was for them. But this right here, *this* is for me."

"Really?" The sudden flush turning her cheeks crimson added spark to her eyes.

He grinned, lifting her slender fingers to kiss her knuckles. "Absolutely. I meant what I said earlier about your movie and if you tell anyone what I'm about to confide in you, I will have to surrender my man card. So please consider your options with the following intelligence."

She propped her free hand on the table, chin in her palm, eyebrows lifted, and made no move to reclaim the hand he'd captured between his.

"I've seen every single one of your movies, not always with a date. Even that Fourth of July picnic farce with the swingers you babysat for." A partial truth. He'd actually seen some of them twice and at least three of them four times and owned every single one on DVD.

Her delighted laughter wrapped around him. The gleam in her eyes tempered the sobriety of her tone. "I promise, your manhood is safe with me."

"Double entendre intended, I hope?"

"Absolutely."

He chuckled, kissing her fingers again and they resumed eating, her hand firmly in his.

The conversation returned to sports.

She preferred basketball to football. He favored baseball and enjoyed basketball enough to debate team statistics.

He liked Italian to her French. She preferred an afternoon at the spa to shopping in Beverly Hills. He was satisfied with the online offerings.

She cited Tahoe as having the best ski resorts. He favored Wisp on the East Coast.

She longed to take a cruise and laughed when he retorted, "My ass rode in Navy equipment enough."

Dinner stretched to dessert and finally to coffee.

They danced.

They laughed.

They talked.

He lost track of the topics, savoring her dry wit, pointed comments, and her absolute failure to agree with him just to agree. She warmed to the areas where they were at odds, favoring Jackie Chan's *Rush Hour* to the clearly superior *Legend of the Drunken Master*. And wrinkled her nose delightfully when he told her it was a good thing she was so pretty.

At two AM, they closed the bar down, but he was content to spend the rest of the night. He hadn't laughed so hard in years.

The irritating buzz of his phone interrupted her suggestion of the local Adolphus hotel and a champagne brunch. He tugged the phone out of his pocket and recognized Damon's number and offered her an apologetic look. He thumbed the phone to answer it. Damon Sinclair was the finest cook he'd ever had the privilege of serving with, considering the man could make potato soup taste like manna from heaven. He also wasn't likely to call James at two-thirty in the morning without a damn good reason.

"Westwood."

"Sorry to cut into your date, Doc. But I'm at the Fillmore with

Matt and there was an incident."

"The Fillmore?" The evening's pleasure drained out of him, his mouth tightening. Matt wasn't ready for bars and shouldn't be off property yet. His gaze cut to the beautiful woman mouthing, '*pub?*' and echoed the question into the phone. "The Fillmore Pub?"

"Yes, sir. Plano cops are here too, sir. I wouldn't call, but Captain Dexter took his fiancée away for the weekend and...."

"No. It's fine that you called. I'm on my way. Can you keep him cool until I get there?"

"Think so, sir."

"I'll be there in...." He glanced at her. She mouthed, *fifteen.* "Fifteen minutes."

"Thanks, Doc."

He rang off and mentally searched for an appropriate apology, but she shooed him out of the booth. He offered her a hand. She slid out and always a marine the flat little purse he'd not seen on the opposite bench.

"I know where it is, so I'll go with you and that way you can get there as soon as possible."

"I'm sorry about this." He felt like an ass, but the waitress appeared to take his credit card and a second brought a light wrap that James helped Lauren into. "I can use the GPS in the car."

"Pfft. GPS. I grew up in Plano. I know exactly where the Fillmore is...." She hesitated, as though taken aback by a thought. "Unless I would be intruding."

"Not at all. I just don't know how long it will take and it's a patient. I need to find out what's going on."

"Then I'll go with you and I'll wait. We can find breakfast somewhere."

He didn't know what to say to that. He definitely didn't want to say goodnight, but without a better idea of what had gone down with Matt, he didn't want to leave her hanging either.

"Tell you what, Marine. You owe me the rest of the night, but I am assuming you're the kind of man who'll let me choose how we spend it."

"Absolutely, ma'am." His eyes crinkled at the crisp notes her voice adopted.

"Then I want to spend it helping this patient of yours, and I expect you to accommodate me." The combination of glitz, glamour, and gritty reality gave him his first true glimpse of the kind of woman she was, not just the woman she played in one of her movies. Combining the tough, no nonsense demand with the artless, charming dinner companion and he found it easy to nod.

He really didn't want the night to end.

He signed the credit card slip and added a generous tip to the waitress' gratuity. Lauren's hand rested in the crook of his arm as they ascended the red velvet steps and exited into the cool September evening.

At the valet stand, he hesitated. She'd driven herself, but she plucked his valet ticket from his fingers. "You can bring me back or I can get a cab...just remember, you'll have me at your mercy and I'm relying on you."

The grin fighting past his concern won out and he nodded slowly. "You are in good hands and I will do everything in my power to live up to your trust."

Her luminescent blue eyes warmed his soul. "I have every faith in you."

He barely noticed the valet taking the slip or returning with his car. Taking care to settle her in the SUV, he slipped the young lady a twenty for bringing the vehicle so fast and paused for a heartbeat to fight the urge to fist pump.

Lauren sat in his car.

She wanted to spend time with him.

What an amazing woman.

"Seatbelt on?" He firmed his grip on self-control and slid into the driver's seat.

The drive to the Fillmore took less than the fifteen minutes she'd advised, but her expert directions didn't allow for a single wrong turn. Three black and white Plano police chargers were angled in the mostly empty parking lot, red and blue lights flashing. He spotted Damon first, talking to one police officer, and searched the stray pools of light for a sign of Matt. The younger man sat on a curb next to his car.

His dented-hood, headlight-smashed car.

"I'll be right back." James gave her knee a quick squeeze and slid out, pulling his Mike's Place ID out of his wallet.

"Sorry, Doc." Damon abandoned the police officer to meet him with a hard handshake. "We just came out for a couple of burgers and beers. It was going fine and then it just wasn't."

"What happened, exactly?"

"You're the doctor?" The officer followed a pace behind Damon, the nameplate pinned to his blue uniform reading Atkins.

"Psychologist." James held out his credentials. "Mr. McCall is one of my patients. What is he being charged with?"

"At the moment, nothing. It's his own car that he damaged and no one is hurt. He settled down some when we got here, but we weren't comfortable letting him drive." The officer looked over the identification briefly before handing it back. He palmed a standard issue flashlight and shone it at the car.

"A brawl started inside, he wasn't a part of it, but apparently they plowed into him. He put both men down, but they're fine outside of some bruises. The bartender and several patrons described the incident and it's a case of self-defense. He could have done a hell of a lot more damage, but he didn't." Respect tinged the officer's words. "Then he came out here and trashed his car. We were already responding to the incident inside when we found him."

James nodded once, flicking a brief look to Damon. "And you don't know why he came out here?"

"No. Like Officer Atkins said, these two guys were arguing, started fighting and they bumped a waitress before they slammed into Matt. I had to hit the latrine or I'd have been right there. As it was, he had one guy down in a chokehold and the other cold cocked on the pool table when I came out. The bartender rounded them up, and the manager rousted them when Matt just walked out of the bar. By the time I got out here, he was kicking the shit out of it."

"Did he say anything?"

"Not a word. Creepiest damn thing I'd ever seen, Doc. It was all surgical strikes, headlights, windshield, side mirrors, tail lights, and then he just beat his fists bloody on the hood. I tried to talk to him when the cops got here. They ordered him to stand down and he did. He's been sitting on that curb ever since...." Damon's words trailed off as he pointed and James followed his gaze.

Lauren was out of the SUV and sitting on the dirty cement curb in her filmy, silk dress, hands clasped in her lap, legs extended with one glittery ankle crossed over the other. Her head tilted toward Matt. Matt looked as poleaxed as James felt when he'd first seen her sitting in the restaurant.

"Thanks, Damon." Worry choked his gut and he headed over. If Matt was unstable, Lauren sat right next to a live powder keg.

Chapter Four

Despite his easy manner, James' palpable tension filled the vehicle all the way to Plano. A professional demeanor, focused concern, and watchful wariness replaced his charming smile and flirty honesty. The desire quivering in her insides sobered in the Fillmore Pub's empty parking lot under the harsh reality of red and blue strobes. He spoke to an officer and a second man dressed in jeans and a T-shirt, presumably the man who'd called him at the club.

She glanced over the others, settling on the young man sitting on the curb. His wide shoulders were framed by a too tight T-shirt that did little to disguise the muscled physique beneath, jeans and scuffed tennis shoes. The close shave haircut coupled with the empty expression on his face and the way he stared sightlessly at the damaged car to his right told her that was who they had been called to help.

Her chest constricted at the loneliness shimmering in the air around him. Dropping her purse on the floorboard, she opened the passenger door and slipped out. The pavement tilted unevenly, littered with cement cracks and blacktop repairs, but she crossed the open space to the young man before she'd fully thought through the decision.

"Do you mind if I join you?" The night air was warm, cooler than the day, but still comfortable. She wrapped her shawl around her more for comfort than heat, holding it firm with the fold of her arms.

The man glanced up, his eyebrows knitting together in confusion. "No ma'am, but I don't really think a dirty curb is going to be kind to your dress."

She chuckled, teetering down carefully to sit and stretch her legs. "That's why I use dry cleaners, they're miracle workers."

The young man continued to stare at her, his confusion giving way to an open bewilderment. "I'm sorry, ma'am, do I know you?"

"Probably not, you're way too young and male to be in my demographic." She extended hand her right hand. "I'm Lauren."

"Matt McCall, ma'am." He took her hand so cautiously she forced herself to stay still lest any motion startle him. His knuckles were black, blue, and red. She'd seen freshly ground hamburger meat that was more attractive.

"It's lovely to meet you, Matt. Are you from Texas?" She considered commenting on his knuckles, but he withdrew his hand far more quickly than he'd offered it and tucked it back down against his leg, out of sight. He wasn't quite rocking back and forth, but the tension thickened in the stiff set of his spine and rigid lock of his jaw.

"No." He gave a quick jerk of his head. "Indiana."

"Really? I've only been to Indiana once." Biting the inside of her lip, she thought back to what James said at the Sybarite Club. People want to be heard. They want someone to listen. And even the most inane piece of trivia can show someone they've been heard. Clasping her hands together, she shifted so her butt wasn't quite perched on the jagged crack in the cement curb. The lazy heat of the day drifted up from warm pavement, chasing away even a hint of chill.

"We were filming a car chase scene that ended in corn fields and then a secondary chase through the fields." Crossing one ankle over the other, she pretended an interest in her painted toes. "Longest week of my life. Corn hurts when you run through it. No one told me that."

"It can be razor sharp, ma'am. I used to hang out in the back of one of those fields with some buddies in high school. We could smoke and talk sh—um—talk stuff about girls and stuff. Anyway, we got to wrestling one day and I got a few good slices."

"So, it's not just me? My director told me it was because I was a klutz, but it's not easy to race through a field, looking over your shoulder and not bang into the plants."

Matt gave her the most peculiar look. "Why was someone chasing you, ma'am?"

"It was in the script. Between you and I, a terrible script. Who runs through cornfields in four-inch heels? I kept losing a shoe or worse, my heel would sink and then I'd trip. But they wouldn't let me just strip them off and drop them to run." The director's high-handed tone still managed to chafe.

"Probably not the best idea to run through a cornfield in bare feet, ma'am. That's a good way to get snake bit."

"Snakes?" A shudder rocked through her and she turned wide eyes on Matt. She didn't have to stretch far to project shock. She hated snakes. Hated them since the episode she'd had to let a python crawl over her when she played Amy Benning, the beloved daughter of Detective Andy. Nasty things.

"Yes, ma'am." Matt's wan smile was still a smile. "Snakes like cornfields, lots of mice to eat."

"Ewww."

He chuckled. A rusty sound if she'd ever heard one.

"Well, I guess I should thank my snotty director for the shoe advice."

"Maybe. But I won't tell if you don't want me to."

"I appreciate that, very much. But enough about me, what's a good-looking young man like you doing, killing time on a curb?"

"Not sure. I don't think they're going to arrest me." The lines of tension around his mouth tightened. "But maybe they should."

"Now why would you say that?" A gamble, she probably shouldn't push. She didn't know Matt, she didn't know his situation, but she knew loneliness when she saw it. She'd seen it in the mirror for twenty years. Isolated, having little contact with her peers and while Hollywood had more than a few child stars, scheduling conflicts and demands left little time for girl talk, mall-hopping or confidences. Add competition for jobs and it just became worse.

"I don't know if I can put it in words, ma'am."

"You know, I say that all the time, or I say that's why I memorize scripts and don't write them. I've been spouting other people's words for years. But if this were a scene in a movie, I'd tell you just to say it plain and let the chips fall. How often do you get a chance to just spit out what's on your mind, to hell with any consequences?" She crossed her fingers and hoped for the right thing to say.

"If you want it plain, ma'am, I'm twenty-four and I'm finished. Done. No prospects. I'm fit, but not fit for duty. I'm strong, but not strong enough. My country needs me, my men need me, and my mama needs me, and I'm no good to any of them." The dull note in his voice worried her more than the statement.

"How are you done, Matt?"

"Inner ear. One little bone. It's cracked. Can't even see the stupid thing and it messes me up sometimes...messes me up enough that the docs wouldn't clear me. The Corps discharged me, honorably, but discharged nonetheless. My guys are still in the sandbox and I'm here, sitting in a bar where a couple of dumbasses get into a fistfight over an order of fries. It's just so damn stupid."

Twenty-four had been a banner year for her. Three movies filmed back-to-back with a fourth script waiting to be memorized. She'd been nominated for a People's Choice at that age.

"It's hard to be told you're done. You can't do what you want to do, what you're good at because of a little bone or the preconception that you can't do it anymore, that you aren't sexy enough or alluring enough to put the butts in the seats. You're good enough to play mom or teacher or nurse, but not to play the love interest or the lead."

Matt blinked at her slowly and she blushed. She was supposed to be listening, not bitching about her career.

"I'm sorry. That kind of just poured out."

"Ma'am, you're way too sexy to be a teacher or someone's

mom. If you'd been my teacher, I'd have paid a hell of a lot more attention in class."

"You're sweet, thank you. But the point I tried to make before I dove off the pier of self-pity is I've been judged by preconceptions since I started in this business. I can try to tell myself it was easy all through my twenties and that those lead roles fell in my lap, but they didn't. First, I had to fight being seen as Amy Benning, and then I had to fight being seen as the quirky romantic comedy lead, and it's impossible to break out of typecasting in Hollywood. I can blame it on my age because thirty-four is dried and done, or I can prove them wrong and fight for the roles I want to fight for, make my own kind of movies."

The thought struck a chord. Take the supporting parts, use the money to fund smaller budget productions or even get a clause in the contract that would allow a contribution. She could take the higher paying empty gigs to pay for those with soul and reinvent herself again. Tucking that thought away for examination later, she focused on Matt.

"Comparing an actress to a Marine...I'm assuming you're a Marine." At his nod, she smiled and continued. "Comparing being an actress to being a Marine is like comparing soufflé to a porterhouse steak, I get that. But you can't tell me being a Marine, going through training, and into combat was easy. It shouldn't be easy adjusting to not serving actively. It's just a different kind of training."

His slow, owlish blink emboldened her.

"And you're a good guy or you wouldn't be sitting here beating yourself up about being sad. But we need to be sad. Sad helps us appreciate happiness and appreciate what we need and what we want. You know what you want, you just have to find a way to do it."

"I do?"

"Of course you do, Matt."

Lauren jumped at James' quiet voice. He'd crept up on them and she'd been so focused on Matt, she'd failed to notice. Blushing guiltily, she shot him an apologetic look, but he held out his hand, a request and offer rolled into one. She accepted the assistance and he lifted her effortlessly to her feet.

"You want to help your brothers. You want to help your family. You just think you can't because the medical discharge papers say your ear inhibits your performance. But that just keeps you out of combat." James' certain, steady voice offered calmness. He squeezed her hand lightly, holding her close and a thrill zinged through her.

Matt climbed to his feet, brow furrowed. "It sounds easy."

"So did basic until the first time you had to run ten miles, do a hundred pushups, then run another ten." Her date's smile twisted with a hint of wryness. "It got easier, but it wasn't easy to start with."

"No, sir. It wasn't." Matt scuffed a shoe against the curb, the deep lines around his mouth and eyes easing. He looked at his car and then back to James, as though really seeing the two for the first time. "I'm sorry, Doc. It won't happen again."

"It's fine, Matt. It's what I'm here for. But you are getting some homework after this."

"Yeah?"

"Lauren." James paused to look at her. "Would you give us a couple of minutes?"

"Absolutely." Turning to Matt, she smiled. "Lovely to meet you, Matt. Thank you for listening."

A faintly puzzled look marred the ghost of a smile flirting with his lips, but still a smile. "Nice to meet you, ma'am...." She made it three steps away when he continued. "And ma'am? If you ever want to try out for Mrs. Robinson, I'll be available."

She swallowed a laugh and gave him a solemn nod. "I'll keep that in mind."

At the car, she dusted off her skirt before sliding back into the passenger seat. James joined her a few minutes later, his features set in a stern expression.

"You're not mad, are you?" She shouldn't have given into the impulse, but he looked so forlorn.

"No." He wrapped his hands on the steering wheel. "I'm not

mad. But that wasn't the safest option. Matt's issues can give him a hair-trigger temper. Staying in the car was as much for your safety as it was his. That said...." He held up a hand when she opened her mouth. "That said, thank you. You listened to him. You heard him. What's more, you made him hear you. That hasn't been an easy road and it's far from over, but he's back on the path and more than ready to be there."

"So I helped?"

"Yes, you did."

She grinned, pleased with herself.

"You're not calling him about a Mrs. Robinson role."

She laughed.

"I'm serious."

"I know you are." She leaned across to brush a kiss to his cheek. "I don't want to play Mrs. Robinson."

"No?" The word echoed on a deep note, low in his throat. She imagined closing the scant inches between their mouths and testing the strength in the firm line of his lips.

"No. I like my man to be confident enough to take on the problems of others, charming enough to admit he liked my films long before he ever met me, and ready to rip out the arms of a man they've never met because he might have pawed me."

"I might know someone like that."

"Yeah?"

He answered with a slow brush of his lips on hers. Gentle, almost fleeting, until her lips parted and his tongue sought access to hers. She cupped his cheek, and the kiss ended nearly as softly as it began. Her stomach fluttered and she opened her eyes, barely even aware that she'd closed them.

"The night's not over yet, James." Definitely time to make some changes, to embrace new challenges and new opportunities, starting with the gorgeous man sitting next to her.

"No?"

She shook her head slowly.

He brushed his fingers over the curve of her jaw. "I live in an apartment at Mike's Place. It's about fifteen minutes from here."

"Fifteen minutes?"

"Maybe twenty if you add the time from car to apartment."

"So twenty minutes?"

"I can make it ten."

"Take your time, we have all night."

Chapter Five

*T*he last thing he'd expected to do when he headed out for dinner was bring his date home, much less invite Lauren Kincaid home. One on level, his brain still tried to wrap around the concept that the actress sat in the passenger seat, hand firmly in his. On another level, he was far more interested in the woman who sat on the curb in her sexy dress and talked to a Marine who desperately needed a friend as easily as she'd charmed James over wine and bad dancing.

The fifteen-minute route through the quiet streets of Plano to the Mike's Place complex in Allen took forever. He considered twice suggesting that they go back for her car, a reasonable alternative to being trapped with his transportation. *But what if she wants her car? What if she decides this is a bad idea?*

Suck it up, Marine.

The gate scanned the identification box attached behind his rearview mirror and swung open smoothly. He obeyed the twenty-mile-an-hour warning signs, vividly aware that a game of touch football at nearly three in the morning was not that unheard of.

"You know, it occurs to me we're breaking the rules." His voice remained remarkably steady considering the triple-time cadence of his heart beat.

"Oh? Which rules are those?" The lazy Texan drawl, barely

discernible in her dulcet tones drifted out to tease him like honeysuckle on a hot summer night.

"Madame Eve's rules."

"She has rules?"

He slid the SUV into its parking spot and cocked an eyebrow at his date. "Yes. Public meetings, fancy hotels, the safety of not being isolated with a stranger...didn't you read the FAQ?"

Her gaze slid to the right. "Small confession time?"

He braced himself. "Go ahead."

"My agent made all the arrangements. I didn't even know there was a site or a FAQ to read."

He laughed. "I see."

"Sorry." She winced apologetically. "If you want to dump me on the side of the road, I understand."

"Oh, I will get over it. But I feel it's important that you understand you have options. I can take you back to your car or take you home. We can go inside, have coffee and talk. Nothing has to happen that you don't want to happen."

Lauren mirrored his pose, unclipping her seat belt to sit sideways. "Are you saying you don't want to have sex with me?"

Good Lord, he enjoyed the woman's directness. "No, ma'am, I'm saying you have options, not that I'm stupid."

Her wide grin cracked through his good intentions. If she got out of the car and walked up the stairs to his place, all bets were off. But he could handle being a gentleman.

For five more minutes.

"Would you like me to be clear?"

"Crystal."

"In the interest of total clarity, I'm going to walk up those stairs, go into your apartment, take off this dress, and ask you to make hot, wet, passionate love to me. If that's all right with you?"

Yep. He adored the little details, like brutal honesty.

He shut the engine off, killed the lights and exited the car to jog around to help her out before she could change her mind. Hand in hand, they dashed up the steps. Her smothered giggles were damn infectious. At the door, he managed to get the key in the lock and open it before remembering he'd left his jacket tossed over the back of the simple dining room chair and a stack of files that he planned to read when he got back.

"One minute?" He grinned and slipped inside to clean up. It took less than thirty seconds to hang the jacket in the coat closet and set the files on the top shelf out of sight.

She laughed when he opened the door fully to invite her in. Her gaze skimmed the room with its sparse furnishings, brown leather sofa, coffee table and lamp, but wasted little time in dropping her purse on the entry table next to his keys and kicking off her heels. Two bookshelves framed the fifty-six inch flat screen and her perusal hesitated.

James kicked himself.

She'd spotted the DVD collection.

Her smile grew wider and her eyes actually teared up a little.

"Hey." Concern overrode the mild embarrassment and he cupped her cheek with his hand. "What's wrong?"

"You were totally serious about liking my movies."

"I couldn't stand most of your movies. I just liked you."

She swallowed. "Wow."

"Truth be told, I don't know that I care about those anymore. The real you is a hell of a lot more interesting than the woman on the screen." He would have said more, but she rose up on her tiptoes and then her mouth was on his. James sealed the kiss, lifting her up and taking his time, tongue delving against her teeth to stroke hers.

He tasted the sweet flavors of coffee and cheesecake and thrust his tongue deeper, trying to capture the decadence of female. Slender fingers dug into his shoulders. Her nose rubbed his, tendrils of her hair teasing his face.

Her breasts rubbed against his shirtfront and as much as he loved the champagne gown, it had to go. Smoothing his hands over the silk, he roamed the smooth swell of her bottom, shaping it until his hands cupped her firmly and lifted her, dragging her sensuous weight up his body. Walking her back to the bedroom, he drew her lower lip between his teeth, nibbling before drifting kisses along her chin to her ear.

"If this is a dream, don't wake me." He tugged her earlobe with a playful nip and entered the sparse space he called a bedroom. The only concession to his exodus from active duty was the king size bed that accommodated his six foot four frame and let him sprawl. A nightstand held his clock and a lamp for bedtime reading, but he hadn't even bothered with pictures on the wall, or a television.

Not that he planned to watch anything tonight. Next to the bed, he set her down, careful not to just shred the dress. Impatience pushed through him and with only the light from the front room slanting across the bed, he rested his forehead against hers.

"Last chance." He wanted to strangle the words. But it never hurt to be sure.

"Okay." She stepped back, running a hand through her hair. "Maybe we should put the coffee pot on...."

Stomach plummeting, he nodded slowly. He'd asked. It was why he asked. It would be too easy to get swept up in the emotion of the moment.

"I'll go get that set up." He turned, allowing enough time to control the disappointment in his expression.

"James." Her voice, coupled with a swooshing sound, halted him. Glancing over his shoulder, his throat locked. The champagne dress pooled at her feet. His gaze rolled over the long, tanned legs, the tapered waist and thin scrap of black and white tuxedo-colored thong, and higher still to the curve of her perfect breasts, small mounds of curvy flesh crowned by pink nipples.

Without the window dressing, she seemed so much leaner, so much more fragile, a goddess carved of delicate coral.

"I thought...." His brain struggled to reconcile her request with the long-legged siren crawling onto his bed to sit on her knees, her delicate eyebrows arched and a mysterious smile on her lips. She crooked a beckoning finger.

"I said you should put the coffee pot on for later...I have a feeling we're not going to get much sleep tonight."

Somewhere the neurons in his brain fired and he toed off his boots, unbuttoned his shirt and stripped the dress shirt and jacket, hanging both on the hook he'd installed next to the closet. He shed the rest of his clothes, never looking away from her. He folded the slacks in half and dropped them over the edge of the footboard.

His cock strained toward her, filled to bursting with the need to make the dream a reality. She studied him with undisguised lust, and he paused at the edge of the bed. She rose up on her knees to welcome him with another searing kiss. Breast to chest, her skin flushed hot against his. She flattened her fingers against his sternum and he leaned forward.

"Stay," she murmured. "I want to see all of you." The shivery words fed the fire in his blood. Fighting the urge to cut the tension with a joke, he let her lean away.

Her lips feathered along his jaw, dipping to nuzzle his throat and teasing a path down his chest. Clenching his fingers, he forced himself to be still, allowing her to explore. Her tongue swirled over his nipple and his cock jerked toward her. He'd never considered his nipples worthy of such attention, but little slivers of lightning dug into his skin, shooting sparks into his brain and flooding his balls with need.

Her nails grazed along his skin, simple caresses spreading tingles. He thrust his fingers into her hair. A glittering, shower of white gold contrasted with the warm honey of her skin. He combed his fingers through it to explore the slender length of her spine.

Her mouth descended, tongue swirling over his belly button. The silken tresses of her hair glided along his cock and his breath clogged in his lungs. Her fingers joined her lips, and she wrapped one hand around him, the other slipping between his thighs to cup his balls.

His knees butted the edge of the bed, and he fought the fierce urge to buck into her fingers. He leaned forward, caressing her back down to the sensuous ass with slender black lace peeking out from the curve of her butt cheeks. His brain dimly registered the presence of the thong, but he teased the lace, edging his fingers beneath to rub her sweet, firm ass with its smooth perfection. The muscles clenched against his fingers and he laughed slowly. Her wet kiss circled the head of his cock and her fingers caressed him.

Thought warred with need. His hips bumped forward, pushing past her lips for a better angle. He glided his forefinger down the length of lace until he sensed the damp heat of her sex and then away again. Her low moan vibrated his cock, and he worried he might come before he was ready. Tiny teeth grazed his flesh gently with every hungry swallow.

"My turn." His voice deepened and he urged her upward and then flipped her onto her back, two fingers tearing away the miniscule tuxedo thong wrapped so lovingly against her sex. The clips snapped and he tossed the scrap of cloth away. He roamed his hands along her breasts, over her belly, and to her thighs. He dropped down to his knees and pulled her ass to the edge of the bed.

One leg slid over his shoulder, and he kissed the inner thigh gently, teeth scraping the tender flesh. He worked his way up to her damp labia crowned by white-blonde curls. Perfection. A goddess laid out for his pleasure, and he intended to pleasure her.

Sparing a look upward, he blew a breath across the sweet, wet sex and dared a single sip. The gasp of her breath offered up a delightful combination of pleasure and encouragement. He teased the lips apart with his tongue. He wanted to play there for hours, but the need raging through his cock wasn't going to allow for much time. Her thighs quivered next to his head as he massaged his mouth across her clit, sucking it in a teasing repeat of her lips on his cock. He vibrated it with his tongue, and her body thrashed around him. The heady smell of her musk filled his nostrils and her sweet cream flooded around his mouth. Bracing her hips, he plundered the flavor, unrelenting until the muscles of her stomach clenched and she cried out again.

Rubbing his cheeks against her thighs, he looked up to see her blue eyes dark with passion and grinned. "Still think we'll need coffee..." He slid onto the bed, urging her toward the center.

"Remind me to tease you every night." But her eyes sparkled with laughter and desire at him. He chuckled. Everything about her beckoned, so unpredictable, sexy, sweet and funny.

He had to write Madame Eve one hell of an endorsement.

Closing the distance, he forgot about conversation, endorsements, files, and the rest of the world. The only thing that mattered was the woman in front of him, the delicious curves that beckoned his lips, and he took his time. His hands explored the smooth lines of her body in between long hot, wet kisses. *So damn petite.*

So many of his first impressions had come from her larger than life personality, her lusty laughs, her teasing glances, and the simple serenity of her chin propped on her hand as she listened to him talk. All of those images collided in his mind, coalescing into the drop dead gorgeous woman perched on that curb.

A fucking amazing woman.

He abandoned her lips to kiss a path down her chest, sampling the warm, vanilla-scented skin. He drew on one turgid little nipple, just barely skimming the tip with his teeth.

"I have a confession to make," he murmured. Her body writhed beneath his while he trailed a damp path to the other breast, intent on lavishing it with the same attention. He could spend the rest of his life right there, teasing the slender body for the soft noises she made.

"Oh?" She pushed the word out on little huffs of breath. He slid his index finger along her slit. The simplest of touches and her body writhed for him again.

"It's been a long time for me."

"Me, too." She arched her hips, but he ignored the demand, settling on her nipple with a swirl of his tongue. Her hips bounced against the bed, one leg rubbing against his arm. He could drown happily in her lush curves, satin softness and silken scent with nothing jagged or hard about her.

"Hmmm," he vibrated his tongue on the nipple, slipping one finger against the slick edge of her entrance. "I think you're teasing me again."

"If I am..." she groaned, "You're paying me back in kind."

He brushed the light stubble of his cheeks against the sensitize tip. Her fingers dug into hair, half pushing, half pulling at him. "I can stop."

"Don't. You. Dare."

"Yes, ma'am." He knew an order when he heard it and captured her lips in a deep, kiss, swallowing any other conversation. He spread the lips of her soaked sex apart with two fingers and fumbled for the condoms he'd dropped on the nightstand. Hardly his smoothest move, but she was so damn responsive, he didn't care.

He swore when he ripped the first one with the foil. Laughing and groaning, she grabbed a second and shuddered around his probing finger slipping in her entrance as she opened it. With control he could only admire, her warm fingers rolled the sheath over his eagerly jerking dick. He met her shy smile with a wider one.

He wanted more time to spread her legs, to dip his head between them, to drive her to orgasm. He wanted to taste her cream and to listen to her cries for release. He wanted to roll her on her belly and take her or lift her into his lap and watch her ride him, but the desire setting fire to his blood ignored all of those wants.

Later. He promised himself.

Reclining against the pillows, she urged him down and then he drove inside her slick entrance and his mind blanked. She was all hot, squeezing tightness and his balls swelled. He fought the rushing orgasm, teasing her clit to bring her with him. He wanted slow and leisurely, but passion pushed at him. They had one night, not enough time to fulfill every wish and desire. He had to try and take it slow, make it as memorable as possible.

He pulled her up and thrust deeper. Her body clamped down on him, her mouth pressed in a silent O against his shoulder. She moaned. The whispery sound allayed any fear that he might have hurt her. He tried to hold himself in check, but his body rebelled against his mind.

His much-lauded control shredded with every glide of her

skin against his. Her nails raking down his back drove him harder and it didn't take him long. She came apart around him, her legs locked around his hips and her low cries gaining volume. He lost it, thrusting deep against the greedy muscles clamping down on his cock and came.

Shaking, he sagged against her, fighting to brace his weight with one arm. Her fingers teased a path up his spine and he grunted, turning his head to look into her drowsy, grinning expression.

"You look stunned." Damn, was there a more beautiful woman in the world?

"I thought I would last a hell of a lot longer." His voice roughened with the confession. He expected to feel embarrassment or shame, but neither emotion sucked him under. Not when he held this woman in his arms.

"I think I would have died of frustration if you'd taken any longer."

"Yeah?" He adjusted his weight for fear of crushing her, but couldn't quite bring himself to pull away.

"Oh, yeah." Her sex clenched as though to emphasize the statement and his body jerked. At thirty-five, he didn't expect to feel his cock stiffening to life so soon, but it did. "I hope you have more condoms...."

"...a whole damn box full, ma'am."

Two hours later, they reclined in the bed and he enjoyed the way her warm skin looked next to his darker, near nut-brown tan from long hours in the sun and too many games of hoops.

"What are you thinking about?" He curled a strand of blonde around his finger.

"That you need more room or a bigger place." She bit down lightly on his shoulder and he arched an eyebrow.

"What for?"

"Honey, we couldn't even fit my shoes in this bedroom...."

He laughed and dragged her beneath him, pausing long enough to roll on a condom before thrusting home in one slow roll of his hips. "You don't need to wear shoes here...or anything else for that matter...."

It was nearly lunchtime when he spotted her sneaking out of the bedroom, dressed only in his shirt, her long bare legs teasing him. They couldn't have slept for more than hour. He stretched, his body stirring at the sight of her bottom peeking behind the tail of his shirt. They'd retreated to the kitchen for coffee and found a way to christen his kitchen counter, the tiny round table he used for work, and his sofa, before making it back to the bedroom.

He wanted to dine on her sweet little sex, again. And again. Maybe he'd offer to cook her eggs and bacon in trade. Her conversation drifted from the front room, derailing the lascivious train of thought.

"Yes, go ahead and work out the details, but tell them I want them to increase the offer by twenty percent, and I want to donate forty percent of the total to Mike's Place in Allen, Texas."

He blinked.

"Yes, I said forty percent. No, I'd like to film all my parts in one week. I have five scenes, surely they can manage that."

His heart sank. One night was not enough. Nowhere near enough. He hoped she'd stick around a little longer.

"Well, it will have to be a week. I'm not going to hang out on set for a month just to film a scene every four or five days. So if they want to film it that way, make sure you include travel expenses. I'm going to be based out of Dallas for the foreseeable future, so it's only a two-hour flight..."

And just like that he blew out a long breath.

"...you know what, Marnie? There's a hell of a lot more to life than just making movies. I'm all about taking chances and seeing where that can go. My career. My life. My choice."

Foreseeable future.

Hell yeah, he could work with that. He levered off the bed, stalked toward the living room and the luscious goddess he planned to lay out on the table.

Time for breakfast.

PROUD TO SERVE HER

HEATHER LONG

ಇಃ

Chapter One

"*N*eeds a cup of Bailey's and a dash of cayenne, John-John." Damon Sinclair handed the large wooden ladle back to an assistant and moved on to check the cornbread coming out of the triple ovens in the back of the bustling kitchen. Opening night hummed in the kitchens with every swing of the doors as waiters and waitresses rushed in, dropped off orders then picked up piping hot food to rush it back out.

Wiping his hands on a towel, he approved all but the last cornbread. "Break that one up and soak it in the red beans." The woman nodded, whirling away with the trays for cutting and adding to the meals, while the last one was passed down to the station chef handling the big pot simmering on one of a dozen stovetops that made up the entire right wall of his kitchens.

Lagniappe's served only the best; if the food wasn't crying to get to the table, it didn't leave his kitchen. He stopped a waitress carrying a large tray, plucked the garnish from a crawfish platter and waved it at John-John. "No weeds with the seafood."

"Aye, Mr. Sinclair." The cook didn't need to call him Mr. *anything*. The aging Marine served the best gumbo in the Quarter. He enjoyed the chaos, and handled it with a firm hand that reminded everyone of the drill sergeant he'd once been.

Damon lured him to *Lagniappe's* with the promise of having

his own kitchen to run. John-John deferred to him as owner, even if Damon was thirty years his junior. Amused, the chef upended the entire parsley garnish onto his cutting board and diced it at high speed before dumping the lot into the Jambalaya. With no garnish to add to the plates, the steward wouldn't make the mistake again.

"Captain Dexter's here." Ginny Mayer sailed in with an empty tray held aloft, neatly dodging Jackson Cooper's heavier load as he carried out a serving tray steaming with cornbread, *étouffée* and gumbo.

"Excellent. I reserved the six-top for them." Damon paused at the dessert counter, studying the beignets with a critical eye. "These are almost too large, you want smaller portions. Remember...each one's a kiss of the south, think brush of the lips, not tongue-thrusting wet."

Demi, the pastry chef, gave him an arch look and worked her mouth into a pout, but the playful gleam in her eyes betrayed her.

"Save the look for the Gunny, Demi. He'll be happy to give you all the tongue thrusting you could want. Give my customers an angel kiss."

"Sir, yes, sir." Her laughter followed him through the kitchen to the doors where he leaned out to look. Immense satisfaction wound through him. It was seven on opening night and every table was populated save for two, one of which he'd reserved for his private guest. *My date who is now,* he glanced at his watch, *thirty minutes late.*

He'd really hoped his hook up from Madame Eve would make it before the rush, but the line out the door coupled with the chatter and laughter making the rounds of the tables filled his soul.

Luke Dexter held a chair out for Rebecca, his fiancée, the stunning chestnut-haired beauty he'd left behind when he enlisted, then won back nearly a decade later. Damon gave the Captain a quiet salute, a gesture the man returned easily. A gasp and sudden rise in volume rolled up the line waiting at the door. James Westwood guided his date, movie star Lauren Kincaid, through the throng of well-wishers. A couple of flashes went off, and Damon slanted a look at Javier the maître d' and nodded his head.

The man diverted from his post to corral the amateur photographers back to their tables with a calm word and a stern expression. *Lagniappe's* wasn't the place for the wannabe paparazzi. James shot him a grateful look, but was quickly distracted when his blonde bombshell pounced on Lauren. The women hugged with a giggling fierceness reminiscent of high school.

They must speak the silent code of the popular.

"You gonna change, boss?" Jones, a waiter, paused at his side, an empty tray dangling from one hand. All of his employees were inactive Marines or related to a Marine. Jones fell in the latter category.

"Soon. Any word?"

"Nope. Javier's checking the line periodically, making sure she doesn't get hung up waiting. But nothing."

Her tardiness annoyed the Marine in him. The schedule called for her to arrive at six-thirty. He took pride in promptness. "Well, I'll change when she gets here. Table seven needs coffee, grab some of the beignets for table fourteen, and bring out two bottles of white for the Captain's table."

"On it." Jones vanished into the kitchens. A wave of oohs and aahs rose from the bar. Matt demonstrated flair with a pair of bottles dancing up in the air. The press of feminine bodies coupled with laughter and applause amused Damon. McCall had come a long way since trashing his car six weeks before. He'd even made plans to spend Thanksgiving with his family.

A big step.

Damon had offered to travel with him, but the man declined. He still received counseling from James regularly, and between the psychologist's support and the rest of the unit, Matt was getting it together.

"Yo, boss...." The call tugged his attention back toward the kitchen, but a tingle on the back of his neck warned him to wait.

Threading through the line at the door was a long-legged brunette, her short dark hair angling around the smooth, alabaster skin of her face. A modicum of makeup—he supposed it was makeup—highlighted fine cheekbones, delicate eyes and a direct, no-nonsense stare that shot a sizzling jolt to his cock.

Oh, please let that be Helena Blake....

Willowy didn't begin to describe the slender woman. A white scarf hung around her neck and dangled between her small, pert breasts. The gray sleeveless top and smart black skirt seemed too sedate for the sensuality in her plump lips and dark eyes. His gaze roamed down her body, pausing only when the crowd surged between them then parted again. The press of people annoyed him, he wanted more than peek-a-boo glimpses.

He watched Javier guide her past the velvet ropes to the private dining area set up just off the main room. Close enough to be public, but private enough to indulge in good conversation.

Hell. Yeah.

Whirling from the door, he darted past the servers to check the white chili with fresh chicken and shrimp bubbling in a separate pot. "Whatcha need John-John...."

∞

Helena eased around the restaurant's overflowing tables. She hated to be late. The maître d' cut a path through, but she had to hurry to keep up or risk the press of bodies refilling the empty space. The overwhelming noise level rattled her after relaxing to Tchaikovsky on the drive. She'd hardly believed the email when it arrived two days ago. Had it really been a year since she'd signed up for Madame Eve's exclusive 1Night Stand service? Had it taken the woman that long to find a possible match?

Skepticism chased the frustration cramping her stomach. Smells assaulted her—first the tang of a fish broil overlaid with the roasting smell of meat, then the sweet pastry aroma of a bakery— all layered together. Her stomach roiled in a vociferous growl. She latched onto each new scent like a drowning man desperate for driftwood. Not eating since the rushed yogurt and protein bar before court had been a mistake.

The rich, piquant scent of gumbo served to the table on her left distracted her, and she bumped into the young man lurching up from the table on the right. She swayed dangerously on her four-inch heels. A firm hand latched onto her arm, steadying her. The maître d' pulled the kid out of her path.

"Thank you."

"Not a problem." But the hard look he gave the poor boy earned her a fast, mumbled apology and an open path through the crowded restaurant to a table segregated by red velvet ropes and carefully placed dividers.

Her escort pulled out a chair for her and she sat, crossing one leg over the other. She hadn't expected to be the first to arrive, particularly since she'd run so late.

"Would you care for a drink?" The man offered no menu or wine list and she pursed her lips. A glass of wine sounded heavenly if not for the small fact that she'd be asleep ten minutes later.

"Actually, I'd love a cup of coffee. Black. No sugar." *Three sugars and loads of cream sounds way better but would add way too much to the hips. So, black it is.*

"Right away, ma'am." Her escort gave her a grin and vanished back into the chaos that was *Lagniappe's*. Elbow propped on the table, she perused the crowd. It was mix of upper middle class to mildly wealthy, sprinkled liberally with college students and young adults. The bar seemed to be the most popular spot, where the ratio of females exceeded the males. The bartender must be something to see.

Exhaling, she stared at a tray of piping hot bread bowls filling a waiter's tray as he ducked through the swinging doors of the kitchen. Her stomach pinched. The carbs alone would kill her diet. Salad would be her best bet, particularly considering her blind date was late. The last thing she needed was to fall on the food like a starving woman.

Another steaming tray of shellfish and cornbread sailed past and she wanted to weep. She'd pay her soul for the spicy combination of crawfish washed down by cold beer. A third man appeared through the swinging doors, and she forced her attention back to the round table in front of her. The heavy red linens on the white cloth added to the atmosphere of city chic meets down home charm. Crystal wine glasses decorated the place settings along with heavy silverware and three cloth napkins per place setting. The restaurant served delicious, messy meals and the napkins would be used.

Except she planned to have a cup of coffee and a salad washed down by water and lemon. Her stomach snarled. She pressed a hand firmly under her rib cage and concentrated on the breathing exercise learned in Yoga. It always got her through a difficult deposition. She couldn't afford to gain any weight. She had a hard enough time getting a date as it was.

Look at me, sitting in the exclusive, isolated spot, waiting for some man as hard up as I am, all to scratch a primal itch that normal people didn't need a special service to arrange. It had sounded so much better in theory.

A cup of coffee appeared in front of her, and she jerked her gaze upward, blinking at the waiter she'd seen exiting the kitchen. Unlike most of the other staff, he actually wore a jacket, the rich black a perfect complement to his dark hair and too-blue eyes.

"Good evening." The rich, rolling cadence of the south drifted through his voice. "One cup of coffee, black."

"Thank you." She closed her cool fingers around the hot cup. She'd barely eaten and had forgotten her suit jacket at the office. The combination of low blood sugar and cooler temperatures left her chilled. "I don't suppose there are menus?"

The waiter's eyebrows lifted. "Yes, ma'am, typically we offer menus." His mouth quirked in an amused smile. "But your meal was prepared tonight by the owner, especially for you."

"I see."

He wasn't a waiter. The fact that he wore a jacket over a button down white shirt and none of the other waiters did was a clue. She couldn't put her finger on it, but she trusted her instincts. No way was he the waiter. So was her date playing a game with her? As her mind raced over the possibilities, her stomach chose the one moment of silence to gurgle. She lifted the coffee cup to her lips to hide her discomfort.

"He planned the meal for six-thirty, but he wasn't sure whether you preferred a white or a red wine and that will tell him a lot about what to serve first."

Oh, he didn't, did he? Well, two can play. She lowered the cup. "My wine selection?"

"Yes, ma'am."

Again with the amusement. What does he know that I don't?

"Wines say a lot about someone. A person who orders a dry white is a focused individual, and prefers clearly defined foods, with a smoky cheese. Whereas the patron who enjoys a fruity white is more likely to indulge in a spicy dish." The lyrical cadence to his words fascinated her.

She rubbed her finger against the warm side of the coffee cup. A swallow of the bitter black brew helped. It was far less than her stomach wanted, but it would have to do for now.

"And red wines?"

"Reds are complicated. First, there are the blushes. The shy palate prefers a blush because she knows what she's getting, but she really wants to experiment. She just doesn't know how. She who desires a merlot possesses sophisticated taste, but is very clear on what she won't try. And Burgundies..." the faux waiter sighed, dragging the word out until the breath caught in her throat. "Burgundies are for those hungry for something they've never had before."

"And you can tell all of that by what wine a person orders?" Her heart thudded against her ribs with a curious thrill of anticipation. If he was the example, this restaurant would be a smashing success.

"Yes, ma'am. Which wine would you prefer?"

"Can you tell what wine a person will order by looking at them?" *Good Lord, I'm flirting with him. Please be the date just playing a game.* Her gaze flicked to the empty seat across the table and back to him. It was a subtle hint, but the man seriously seemed to notice everything. His blue eyes were amazing, but he didn't seem to take the hint.

All the noise and chaos behind him faded as he leaned in with a secretive smile. "Sometimes."

"Surprise me." She nibbled her lower lip, probably scraping what was left of her lipstick off, but she didn't care. He wasn't looking at her mouth. Correction, the waiter wasn't looking just at her mouth. Instead, he seemed to take in her whole body and she straightened, almost self-conscious of the appraisal.

"I'll do that." He circled the table to retrieve a napkin and snapped it out to lay over her lap. The move was so at odds with the location and yet utterly charming nonetheless. "My name is Damon and it will be my pleasure to serve you tonight."

He winked and pivoted neatly to disappear behind the swinging doors. She exhaled sharply, her skin tingling all over. Her pulse raced like a wild hummingbird. Heat uncoiled in her belly.

He had to be Madame Eve's date. She wasn't sure why he wanted to pretend to be the waiter, but he was really cute at it. She told herself that the flutters in her belly and the stuttering of her heart had nothing to do with her decision to continue to play along.

Chapter Two

*H*e marched through the swinging doors, bracing one open for the line of waitresses carrying full trays out. "John-John, did we get in those sides of beef we ordered?"

"Yes, sir." The chef gave him a squinty-eyed look from behind the silver racks in front of him. "What's on your mind, Mr. Damon?"

Letting go of the door as the last waitress passed, he considered the whole of the kitchen. Every pair of hands was engaged in some activity, every dish in some stage of preparation. "Filet cuts, two butterfly cut and two half-inch thick. burgundy red, and au jus for the butterfly, on a bed of ice-chilled lettuce with a crumble of the cornbread. Coffee-rub the half-inch thick filets with chicory and the sweet Columbian, slow cook to medium with the ends done to medium well."

"Not bloody."

He shook his head slowly. "She's a little skittish for bloody. Sweet potato soup, add some of the cubed Idahos to it, pinch of salt, dash of paprika. Quarter up the vegetables and steam them over the gumbo and grilled shrimp as a garnish."

"You got it."

Damon left him to it and circled through the kitchen to the wine vault, itself a work of art—hand carved shelves, temperature controlled, no humidity and a level of low lighting that let him read the labels without harming the wine. He trailed his fingers along the bottlenecks, tugging out one or two with a thought for the leggy beauty.

She thinks I'm the waiter.

A grin tugged his lips. He probably should have outted himself, but the unease in her expression relaxed during their conversation. A spark of amusement had flooded her dark eyes and he wanted to see more of that.

It would be no problem to serve her. If the night went well, she would need all the calories he could give her.

He paused and contemplated a label. Satisfied, he pulled out a bottle. *Perfect.*

Shutting down the lights, he stepped back into the coordinated chaos of his kitchen, letting the laughter and the camaraderie wash over him.

"Demi, you got time to put together a selection of bread and cheese, skip the crackers, use the thinner slices of the pumpkin, nine grain, cornbread with the *bleu*, the gouda and that creamy Swiss we picked up?"

His bakery chef grinned and gestured to the tray of fresh beignets. "Do I need to kiss those, too?"

"Air kisses are good." Winking at her, he twisted the corkscrew into the bottle top, popping it open to breathe. He watched her movements with a critical eye, approving or disapproving of Demi's selection until she set up the rectangle trencher, five thin slices of bread, each boasting a bit of cheese. She added a raisin to the bleu cheese, a dab of peach jam to the side of the Swiss and sliver of apple to the gouda.

"Perfect." Lifting the rectangle, he pushed through the doors to carry the wine and cheese platter to his date. She was staring at a smartphone in her palm, finger tapping away. He navigated through the crowd and the velvet rope to their private little nook apart from the noise. In one smooth move, he slid the cheese platter onto the table and plucked the phone from her hand.

"Hey!" Her smooth forehead knitted together. She lifted her

chin, a spark of outrage flushing her pale cheeks with color. He highly approved of the glow warming her face and pressed his thumb to the power button without looking at the screen.

"No cell, smart or mobile phones allowed, ma'am." Southern apology drifted under the words, not that he experienced an ounce of remorse. It might be controversial and elitist in some parts of the country, but he believed work disturbed a meal. His customers came to *Lagniappe's* for the experience and the sign added to that ambience. Typically, he didn't enforce it, but he wanted her attention focused on the meal and on him. "They're bad for digestion."

"And if I was sending a text message to my daughter?"

Damon paused, considering her pinched expression. "Were you, ma'am?"

She sighed. "No, I was answering a message from my assistant."

"Then it can wait until after your meal." He slipped the phone into his pocket, ensuring that she would stick around for the rest of his plans rather than get irritated and leave.

She stared at his pocket, but didn't protest.

He presented the bottle of wine with a smile. "May I present your wine choice for this evening, a 1972 *Châteauneuf-du-Pape*? Made from thirteen types of grapes, it is spicy, with a combination of black and red raspberries and soft on the palate. It is both sweet and dry." Cradling her wine glass between his fingers, he poured a small sample and watched her frown melt away at its rich ruby color.

"You chose a burgundy for me."

"A grenache, but close to burgundy." He appreciated her delight and held the glass out, enjoying the way her cool fingers brushed his to take it.

Setting the bottle down, he shuttled aside her coffee cup. "What we have here is a selection of cheeses, some smoky, some sweet. Each comes served on a thin bed of bread. Bread is better than crackers because each flavor will spark another. I would suggest that you begin with this pumpkin slice, with bleu cheese and the raisin. They are cut so that you eat each one whole, allowing the flavors to dance on your tongue."

She rolled the wine in the glass, her expression rapt as he explained, her attention dipping to the plate and back again. Hesitation made her smile hitch. "I've never been a fan of bleu cheese."

Damon crouched next to her chair. "It's not about like or dislike. It's about teasing your palate, allowing you to experience the flavors. The pumpkin and the raisin bring out different aspects of the aged cheese, each allowing the other to tell you a different story. The pumpkin is autumn fresh, new and brazen. The aged cheese is like the wine, it takes on elements of experience while the raisin is both sweet and tart, giving the bleu a new lease on life."

Her white teeth pulled on her lower lip and he wanted to run his tongue over her pouty, pink mouth, tug it with his own teeth and then feed her. But it was best to go one step at a time. Like the cheese and the wine, she needed to acclimate, to sample and let the food bring out new layers.

And he could sample them all.

She seemed to lose some inner struggle and laughed. It was a gorgeous sound. "I don't think I've ever heard anyone talk about food this way before."

"Too many people treat food like fuel. Firing up to rush from one place to the next. I get it. I've been there. But I can enjoy it now. Would you allow me to show you how?"

She smothered her laughter and the hint of color in her cheeks flared again. He liked keeping her off balance. He nodded to the plate. "Choose the pumpkin bread and try that with the cheese."

He wanted to make the selection and offer it to her himself, but he was still playing the role of waiter. She hesitated, but reached for the pumpkin bread square and lifted it to her mouth. Anticipation curled in his stomach as her lips parted.

"Close your eyes, take a small breath through your nose. Let the smoky combination tease your palate and then taste with your tongue." He wanted to follow the path of that bread and kiss her with the flavor warm on her lips, but he forced himself to remain still.

A hint of rebellion slipped through her gaze, followed by the barest sensation of impatience. Impatience for him or impatience for herself, he wasn't sure, but her lashes fluttered down and her nostrils flared. She slid the bite into her mouth.

She was still for several seconds before gliding her lips against each other as though savoring the flavors and a mild ecstasy rippled across her expression.

Her eyes popped open, surprise and delight filling them. She pressed two fingers to her mouth. "Wow."

"Indeed. Now sample the wine, a careful sip, just enough to let it swirl through the flavors already on your tongue." How he envied the wine as the crystal touched her lips and she took a small drink. The color in her cheeks deepened, flushing to a healthier pink that heightened the sparkle in her eyes.

"Good?"

"Amazing." She held the glass away, looking at it with wonder and then inspected the plate with a curiosity that filled his soul to satisfaction. "They're all different."

"Of course. Each one has a different story, a different experience waiting for you to discover." He stood slowly, reluctant to continue the game and disappointment flashed across her face.

"I should probably wait for my dinner date." A forlorn note creased the words. "I thought he would be here by now."

"Then it is his loss for being late. But you have another course coming and we can easily prepare him anything he wishes. Don't let his absence rob you of this opportunity." He promised to kick the crap out of himself later if this backfired, but the air of loneliness around the woman diminished. She'd thought he was the waiter and he'd intended just a little bit of fun, but watching her rapture over the food, the careful way her teeth grazed her lips, and how she savored the wine were doing wild things to his cock.

He wasn't sure she'd allow such abandon with her *date*.

She set the wine glass down with determination. "You know,

you're right and I am now very curious about the rest of this cheese."

"That's my girl." He grinned. "I'll be back in just a few minutes."

ഗ്ദ

The sucking black hole of loneliness enveloped her with his absence. It was odd how delightful the restaurant sounded, the musical notes straining through the hum of the crowd, the swish of the doors, the clink, clank of the plates and the bursts of explosive laughter. The symphony descended into cacophony when her "waiter" vanished back into the kitchens. Helena sighed, swirling the burgundy—grenache—around in the glass. He'd brought her the burgundy, the wine for the hungry soul. *How did he describe it? Burgundy wine drinkers are hungry for something they've never had before?*

She sampled more, letting the wine flow around her tongue. It was spicy and fruity and gentle, all the things Damon described.

And the seat opposite her was still empty. Because she was hungry for something she'd never had before. She was hungry for a real connection, something both physical and intimate, but without the tangle of strings or the dating dance which was near impossible to meet on her schedule—and had been for more than a decade if she was honest with herself. Sometime between graduating high school at sixteen and entering college on an accelerated program that earned her a bachelor's degree before she was nineteen, she'd forgotten how to have fun. If she wasn't studying, she was working, if she wasn't working she was sleeping, and then only in small increments. She was thirty years old and she had just received the offer to become a full partner in her law firm.

She should be out celebrating with friends, except her closet friend preferred his meals served on a plate in the kitchen and then to snuggle on her law briefs while she tried to review them.

Of course, what do I know? I think my date is playing waiter tonight, and I'm not sure why. But it's fun and a little naughty.

She inspected the thin slice of nine grain with the Swiss layered over the top and a drizzle of honey for flavor. Her last date had been to junior prom, which somehow didn't seem to count in the great, grand scheme of things. A wild burst of laughter from the crowd dragged her away from the melancholy.

Thankful for the distraction, she bit into the hors d'oeuvre. The flavors melded together, blindingly sweet, tart, with something as familiar and homey as the wheat. The bread's texture was grainy compared to the utter smoothness and she chased bits around her mouth, sliding them against her teeth before swallowing.

She washed the mouthful down with wine and a flush of guilty pleasure. She wasn't supposed to play with the food. A glance at her watch said it was nearly twenty to eight and her date was still a no show.

Pausing mid reach for her purse, she frowned. Damon had taken her cell phone. She couldn't even check to see if Madame Eve sent her a note that something else had come up.

Impatience flashed through her and she scooped up another piece of cheese and bread. She'd have to double her time on the treadmill tomorrow to begin to make up for the calories she was indulging in. But hell, it was her birthday, she'd been stood up by the so-called perfect one-night stand and she'd rather devour the sweet cheese and fruity wine than all the self-pity in the world.

A shadow drifted across her plate and she glanced up, half-ready to give the latecomer a piece of her mind, but her *waiter's* raised eyebrows stilled the acidic words. The corner of her mouth turned up and she set the wine glass down.

"I take it you didn't like that piece."

If she could bottle his accent and intonations, she could sample them every day. "No...I mean yes, it was fine. I don't think I really tasted that one, I was too busy being a bitter old bat."

With practiced ease, he slid away the trencher of cheese and bread and replaced it with a round plate featuring crisped greens and the most sinful piece of steak. Her stomach recovered from the doldrums faster than her smile. The scent of wine lingered in the air, along with traces of beef and a mouthwatering spice she couldn't quite put a finger on.

"First, we do not insult ladies in this establishment, so no more *bat* comments. Second, if you're bitter and old, you must introduce me to ancient and decrepit." The confident ease in his voice did more to stroke her ego than all the pretty compliments in the world. For a horrifying moment, tears touched the back of her eyes and she blinked them away.

"Thank you."

"You're welcome." But instead of abandoning her to the next course, he set out her silverware and traded the black napkin for a red before squatting down, one hand braced on the back of the chair.

"Would you like to tell me what's wrong?"

Mortification vied with attraction and she shook her head. *Do you want to confess to being my date now? Because at this point, if you're not, I have a feeling my date is going to be dramatically disappointed. Or I am.*

"No, I'm sure you have a lot of better things to do than listen to me moan and complain."

"Actually, there's nothing better I have to do than listen to your complaints, particularly if I can fix them. As for moaning, just give me time. I promise, I can't wait."

Shock and awe rolled through her, but she wasn't sure which one was winning. It was one thing to flirt with the truly good-looking waiter, his lean build and well-muscled physique a testament to his fitness, but it was something else to think he was flirting with her.

God, do I have to be so rusty at this? Is he actually flirting or am I just looking for crumbs?

"Seriously." He laid a hand over the top of hers. "Tell me what's wrong. I promise you, if I can fix it, I will."

Her throat choked up and she blinked back the mortifying assault of tears burning her eyes. This was exactly why she'd needed a Madame Eve, because she could light her competition up in the court room, but she'd never figured out how to capture that sizzle outside of it. "I was supposed to be meeting someone tonight, but I was late and obviously they are too or they didn't bother to show up. It's my birthday. I've been looking forward to tonight for the last week. I hadn't really thought I had been and then everything went kerfuffle in court, and the judge was a pain in the ass, and I couldn't get out of there on time, and it looks like I'm spending my birthday eating this beautiful food alone. So pity party, table for one." The words poured out like a wound lancing open, the pressure on her chest eased, and the cramps in her legs relaxed.

She glanced away from Damon. She was not going to turn into some hysterical female bawling all over him because she'd been stood up.

"It's your birthday...." His words were slow, mesmerizing and drew her gaze back in spite of herself.

"Yes. The big 3-o. Happy birthday to me...I don't suppose your boss would let you join me for the meal?" She had no idea where the sassy invitation came from, but once it slipped past her lips there was no taking it back.

"Even if he didn't, there's no place else I'd rather be." He smiled slowly, almost hesitantly. "About your date...."

"No." She cut him off by turning her hand over under his and indulging in the contact, no matter how brief. "I don't want to talk about him. He's not here. Let's just leave that plot buried, shall we?"

He threaded his fingers with hers. She liked his hands, the fingers were tapered, strong and evenly callused. Whatever he did for a living, he used his hands and he used them well. She half-wondered what it would be like to have them touching her, but immediately shuttled that into the inappropriate and creepy bin. Poor guy was probably just being nice to the hysterical customer.

"I would love to join you for dinner."

Surprise flared in her. *Seriously?*

"I don't want to get you into trouble." She tried to withdraw, but his grip subtly tightened.

"No trouble at all. In fact, I should have from the start. Now...." He pressed a kiss to her knuckles and his sexy blue eyes locked on hers. "Give me three minutes and we're going to have the best birthday dinner you've ever eaten. I promise."

"Three minutes?"

"And not a minute longer."

He released her, rose to his feet and scooped up the cheese plate in one smooth motion. With a wink, he pivoted and headed off to the kitchen. *Did he just confess to being my date?* Hope flared in her stomach. She didn't like the indecision or the worry. *You know, to hell with it. Whether he's my date or not, he's joining me.* She saluted her new resolve with another mouthful of wine.

She really was hungry for something she'd never tried before....

But somehow she doubted that Damon was on *Lagniappe's* elusive menu.

Chapter Three

*H*e snapped into the kitchen, moving double time, a man on a mission. "Mindy, trade stations with Jan. I want you working the tables closest to the private lounge. You're going to take over bringing out the dishes. John-John has the orders and he'll give them to you when they need to be delivered."

"Um, okay." The redhead arched both eyebrows. "I thought that was your table."

"It is. Hit the privacy curtain, time to see if the money I spent on that was worth the investment. And switch over the tracks to Blue Star."

"Jazz trio?"

"Yes." He swung by John John's station, eyes skimming the marinating steaks. "Thirty more minutes on those. Sweet potato soup first and get Demi to hollow out some of those sweet potato breads for bread bowls."

"You said those were too sweet." John John didn't look up, but amusement littered his words.

"Pinch of salt and paprika on the soup should offset that. Send those out in fifteen. Steaks in forty-five."

"Yes sir, Mr. Damon. I'll be sending." Despite the sardonic *Driving Miss Daisy* humor, the chef spared him a reproachful look. "It's about time you sat down with that young lady and stopped playing games."

"Not changing strategies." Guilt punched him. Should have just 'fessed up so she didn't feel stood up. He didn't realize it was her birthday. He was such an ass. But he could fix it. "Just moving up the time table."

Salad plate in hand, he exited the kitchen. The crowd continued to ebb and flow. Captain Dexter's table had added four more chairs and he caught the hand wave from Logan and the nod from Zach. It didn't surprise him that his fellow Marines made a show of solidarity, but it did leave him with a satisfied glow. They never left a buddy behind and tonight was no exception.

The curtains were already rolling around the private lounge, the swish of heavy velvet a whisper against the tiled floors. He caught the fabric, letting himself in before it closed then drank in the sight of her parted lips, raised eyebrows and wary pleasure—he was going to have to do something about that wariness.

Setting his filet and salad on the spot next to hers, he shifted the table settings and pulled up a chair. He checked his watch—sitting right at the three-minute mark.

"Are you sure you're not going to get into trouble?" Her voice was a smooth contralto, a perfect descant to his deeper voice, and wholly feminine.

"I'm positive. And it would be a crime to leave you sitting here alone." He shook out the napkin, spread it over his slacks, and glanced at her plate. She'd left it be, exactly as he asked and he considered it for a moment, switching the plates so hers boasted the warmest steak on the coldest salad.

Shifting in her chair, she crossed one leg over the other and he fought the urge to glance down. The tip of one black heel peeked out from under the tablecloth, flashing a sexy, come-hither red bottom at him.

"Thank you and I apologize. I should not have dumped all of that on you."

"I asked. I wanted to know." The corner of his mouth tilted up at the wash of emotion dancing across her face—confusion, regret and a hint of exasperation. "Tonight is supposed to be special for you. I've picked a wide selection of dishes designed to tease and tantalize your palate, and none of them come with a side of misery."

"I thought you said the owner chose my menu tonight...." The slow delivery suggested she'd already put the pieces together, so he refilled her glass before adding a generous measure to his own.

"I did."

"You own *Lagniappe's*?" Her lips parted in expressive wonder.

God, he hoped she was as delightfully open when he carried her off to bed. It was going to be a lights-on session, all hands on deck and his eyes on hers when he slid between her thighs. His cock jerked hopefully at the thought, but he ignored the urge to jump the gun. Strategy was about surgical insertions and definitive results. They'd not finished prepping the foundation yet.

Soon.

"Yes, ma'am. Damon Sinclair at your service and as I said earlier, it is my pleasure to serve you. Now, shall we drink to new acquaintances and new experiences...?"

Her eyelashes fluttered twice and her lips stretched into a grin that promised delight. "Helena Blake, Mr. Sinclair."

"*Damon.*"

"Damon." She touched her glass to his, the gentle clink an almost musical note. "To new acquaintances and experiences."

He watched her sip before taking one of his own, testing the flavor with a swish of his tongue. The *Châteauneuf-du-Pape* was an excellent vintage, its spicy undertones warming his mouth. A soft sigh pushed past her lips and he smiled again.

"You like the wine."

"I *love* the wine." She set the glass down with a little shiver. "But I'm not much of a drinker, not sure I could tell you the difference between a boxed variety, or a fine vintage. But this is magnificent."

He barely held back the grimace at the mention of the boxed variety.

"What?" Her soft brown eyes narrowed and the glass lowered to the table. "You said you could tell a lot about a person based on the wine they drank. What does a box wine say about me?"

"You're going to make me answer before I can coax you into trying this next dish, aren't you?"

Releasing the glass, she sat back in the chair, arms folded. "Yes, I am. Because now I'm really curious."

"You shop at a Kroger's or an Albertson's on your way home from the office. It's always late when you swing in there, you always have work to do, and a box will keep for days if you need it to. You probably choose the zinfandel because it's sweet, and if it's an indulgence, then it should be sweet." He cleared his throat and gave her silverware a pointed look. She reached out for the fork and sat forward, posture relaxing.

Nodding with approval, he continued. "You carry it back to the Styrofoam palace housed in your fridge. You probably drink it in a mug that you can rinse out and have fresh coffee in if you have to work late. But you have your cup while eating cold noodles from a dinner two days before and working at the kitchen counter."

Yes. He could totally envision that.

Her mouth opened and closed. "I'm not sure whether to be impressed or terrified."

"As I said, wine says a great deal about a person. But you are not dining at your Styrofoam palace, you're having dinner with me."

Her wariness gave way to a flash of trepidation that vanished under a wider smile. "I am, aren't I?"

"Yes, and about your date...." Time to come clean, fantasy or no fantasy. It was her birthday and what began as a fanciful tease wasn't fun anymore.

She cut him off with a wave of her hand. "No. Let's not. I'm really enjoying this...now...just the way it is."

His conscience argued against the idea, but she looked so pleased that he was hard-pressed to push the issue. It was dinner.

It's her birthday....

"Very well, it's your birthday. We'll do it your way." He turned away from the niggling worry of common sense and focused on the fantasy. "Now, what you see in front of you is a filet, butterflied thin and cooked slowly with red wine. A burgundy." He emphasized his earlier selection and grinned at the warm sparkle in her eyes. "And *au jus*, allowing the meat to absorb the flavors of both as it's slowly turned on a low fire. The lettuce is romaine, cooled to thirty-eight degrees to preserve freshness. The idea is to slice into the steak, spear a small section along with the lettuce and to bite into both simultaneously."

He demonstrated, spearing a sliver of his steak with one crisp lettuce section and leaned toward her, fork aloft. His gaze never left hers as her mouth parted beautifully, accepting the offering and he glided the meat home to her tongue. His abdomen tightened as her lips closed on the fork and she took the whole bite.

Her low groan lacked any hint of artifice or drama. Instead, her eyes shimmered, surprise filling them. With two fingers to her lips, she chewed and spoke at the same time. "Oh, my God...."

"The steak is rich, but the lettuce is cool, it's an assault. Save the wine for when you are done, or it will change the flavor subtly on your palate."

"I've never had anything like this before...."

"That's why tonight is all about new experiences." She picked up her knife and fork and began to cut into the steak. The echoes of Blue Star's experimental melodies rolled into the quiet air around them, muting the hum of the restaurant beyond the heavy curtains.

Yes, sitting down to dinner had been the best plan. Her pink tongue flicked out to catch every morsel of steak.

He couldn't wait for the next course.

ര

In very fine restaurants, and she'd eaten in enough of them, the salad didn't come until after the meat, and the cheese typically came after that. But nothing about this evening or the meal, seemed to be following what she would normally expect. By the time the hedonistic steak and salad course was swept away and a bread bowl laden with soup was set before her, she didn't care.

She immersed herself in the evening, in her pretend date with the waiter, and the wildly delicious food. It was past eight, she should be home reviewing case files, but Judge Albert was going to issue a continuance in the morning no matter how prepped she was, the plaintiff's case wasn't ready and her client had been dealing with nuisance suits for years.

Damon poured a third glass of wine and gestured to the bowls. "Sweet potato bread, cooked hard, cored out to serve as the bowl for sweet potato soup. There're diced Idaho potatoes with a dash of paprika and a pinch of salt for flavor. The soup is a palate refresher, it will relax your taste buds and prepare them for the next course."

She loved the way he talked about the food and didn't hesitate to dip her spoon for a taste. The soup was rich and creamy with a hint of sweetness, but to her utter surprise she could taste the paprika.

"You like?" He swirled the wine in the glass, leaning back in the chair. He'd angled his seat until they were sitting closer together. The stretch of his long legs beneath the table warmed hers and she'd compensated to sit slightly twisted, taking advantage of her front row view. He really was the whole delicious package from the white shirt contrasting with his olive complexion. Although not a huge man, the elegance and precision in his movements emphasized his musculature.

And then there were his eyes.

She'd never understood the phrase 'drown in his eyes' until she was able to feast on the sight of his. They were the most perfect shade of midnight blue. The sound of the restaurant beyond the curtains might as well have been miles away for all that it failed to intrude on their intimate tête-à-tête.

"If I forget to mention it later," she murmured, "I think this is my favorite birthday."

He grinned and her pulse thudded. "We've just gotten started, don't give away the prize until the mission is complete."

Laughter bubbled up and she took another spoonful of soup, her gaze skating over to watch his hands as he began to eat. His expression was neutral as he sampled the flavors.

"It's not quite perfect. I think we should have added the Idaho potatoes later."

"I think it's wonderful. But now I am very curious."

"And what are you curious about?"

"You know so much about food and you obviously enjoy it, but why a restaurant? There's so much more to running a restaurant than just the food." She'd seen the unfortunate results of what happened of creative passion overwhelmed by the demands of running a business. It wore a person down. In at least two cases, she'd seen those same passionate people lose their appetites for creating altogether because the work of ownership carried too much pressure.

"My mother was passionate about food. She believed in the family table, the breaking of bread and the joy of serving. Every Sunday, we came home from church and she'd serve food, the neighbors came over, and brought dishes with them. You could always find food at our house. Saturday nights were always about the preparation. It was a party to stand in the kitchen, sampling the different flavors, putting together the combinations. Even when the steel factory layoffs came and Dad was out of work, she could turn potato and leek soup into an experience. 'Damon,' she would say, 'food is for the soul. Your belly only thinks it is in charge. Never let hunger determine your meal.'"

"That sounds amazing." Her parents favored microwaveable meals in front of the television or she ate at her desk in her room as she pored over her books. They'd never dragged her away to *experience* a meal, often as not, leaving her to study when they went out to meals and bringing her back some take out. "I can't imagine spending hours cooking. My culinary skills extend to opening a pot pie box and nuking it for five minutes."

"And why don't you cook?"

"You think all women know how to cook?"

"Absolutely not. One of the women in my unit burns water and a buddy of mine pays his wife not to cook because he's had food poisoning twice." His quick grin lit her own and she couldn't help the laughter.

"That's awful."

"But true. So no, I don't *expect* a woman to know how to cook. But why didn't you learn?"

She glanced down at the nearly empty bread bowl and wondered if it would be impolite to begin to nibble on the soup-soaked bread. As though reading her mind, he reached over and tore off an edge, drenched it in the creamy bottom and held it up to her lips.

She caught his gaze as she took the offered bite, her tongue just barely grazing his finger, but he didn't pull away, instead, catching a stray drop sliding over her lower lip and offered it to her. Boldness flooded through her and she drew his finger into her mouth until she cleaned off the drop.

"You were saying?" The hint of teasing drifted along the thick undertones of his voice and she sighed.

Yep. No matter how this evening ended, it was definitely the best birthday ever.

"I was something of a prodigy when I was younger. By the time I was seven, my parents had to enroll me in a private school and I skipped several grades. By the time I was twelve, they hired a private tutor because I was a freshman in high school. I graduated at sixteen, but only because my mother was reluctant to allow me to graduate at fifteen. I finished my Bachelor's in Criminal Justice at nineteen and law school a month before my twenty-second birthday. I've been an associate at my law firm since then, and I just got offered partner last week. I haven't had time to look at anything except books or legal briefs."

His expression dimmed at her sigh and she fought for a smile.

"I'm whining and I'm aware of that. I never really paid attention to anything else, it's not that I was denied the opportunities, I was just...."

"You were focused. You had an objective. I get it. I skipped the college experience. Went straight into the Corps the day after I graduated high school. Family tradition. My grandfather, my father. My great-grandfather was a Navy man. My uncle was in the Army, and I have a kid brother who went Air Force, something about liking to play with his stick."

A shiver washed through her at his easy grin.

"So you were a Marine...."

"No, ma'am. I *am* a Marine. I'm just not on active duty." He picked up his wine glass and she mirrored him, barely aware of the waitress stealing away their plates and replacing them with a platter of steak and steamed vegetables. The scents creeping up from the plates set her mouth to watering and her stomach cheered.

Unless she planned to spend eight hours on the treadmill the next day, she'd never burn off so many calories.

"Thank you, Mindy." He never lifted his gaze from Helena's and her cheeks began to ache from smiling, the muscles of her face locked in a permanent grin.

"Yes, thank you." She managed a quick glance at the waitress who winked and slipped away as quietly as she'd come. The parting curtain revealed dimmer lighting beyond and the haunting blues of a lone jazz horn.

"Oooh, you have live musicians, too." Her heart did a little fist pump. She'd had one case take her to the French Quarter a year before, just a week after her birthday and a street musician's performance brought her to tears. She'd never heard such a mournful, beautiful sound before.

"Yes, ma'am. Would you like me to tell you about your dinner?"

"You can tell me anything you want. I'm completely in your hands." Apprehensive desire knotted in her belly. It was the single, most provocative thing she'd ever said to a man and the intensity flaring in his blue eyes told her he'd received the message, loud and clear.

"Completely?" he asked, setting the wine glass to the side and plucking hers from her nerveless fingers.

"Completely."

Tingles followed the brush of his skin on hers and she held her breath. "Will you let me feed you?"

"Haven't you been doing that already?" The one-two punch of her heart against her ribs sounded so loud in her own ears.

"Yes, but I want to give you the full experience. I want you to close your eyes and keep them closed...let me feed your soul, one bite at a time."

Heat flamed between her thighs and her panties dampened. Not quite trusting her voice and not altogether certain it was the best idea, she nodded slowly.

He traced his fingers across the palm of her hand. "Close your eyes."

She gazed at him for a long moment, burning an imprint in her mind of his intense expression, earnest gaze. Clenching her fingers into her napkin, she closed her eyes.

"How is your palate?" The words shivered through her, and he abandoned her palm to stroke her cheek. She hoped he never stopped.

"I don't know. I think it's...I think it's okay. Everything has tasted wonderful."

"Let's see." His breath whispered against her lips, the warmth of him washing over her face. Her eyelids fluttered, but a brush of his fingers kept them closed.

The first touch of his lips on hers and she forgot to breathe. His lips were soft, warm and her mouth opened in a silent O. Her thoughts fogged. Electricity raced down her spine. His tongue rubbed against hers, an invitation. She forgot to think altogether.

Chapter Four

$\mathcal{H}$er mouth opened willingly beneath Damon's. What began as a provocative tease, escalated to explosive passion. She kissed with an almost shy, abandon that rang a chord deep inside him. He forgot about the food, teasing her palate, and the game of seduction. The earthy, rich, sweet scent of her filled him. Need raged through him and his pants tightened a notch. The desire to take it slow and explore warred with the want to strip off all their barriers and claim her right there on the table.

Her head fell back and he smiled and coaxed her tongue back against his own lips, sucking sweetly and delighting at her first tentative thrust against his teeth. Cradling her face between his hands, he drew lazy, slow circles with his thumbs against her cheeks. He wanted her boldness. He wanted her to demand. Hell, he wanted to answer those demands.

Inch by inch, her body shifted in the chair, turning in toward him until a length of her bare leg brushed against his pants and the fire he teased roared to life. A low moan seemed to roll up from her belly and then her hands were in his hair, nails lightly scraping against his scalp. The push-pull thrust of their kiss dropped a live grenade of lust in his belly, detonating until his cock swelled painfully.

Her shudders dragged him back from the decadence of her lips. Breaking the kiss, he glided his fingers along her arms, and tugged her fingers away from his hair until he could cradle both of her hands in his. Her eyelashes fluttered open revealing glazed passion in her eyes. No trace of nervousness remained in her expression. Her sexy, sweet swollen lips—plumped from one, sinfully delicious kiss—quirked into a grin.

"How was my palate?" The sassy comment was so at odds with her thready whisper.

"Hungry." That was not the word he intended to use, but it fit. This was a woman who needed to be kissed and kissed often. Thank God those words didn't fall from his lips, but too many viewings of *Gone With the Wind* at his mother's house and Rhett's effusive declaration to Scarlett fit.

Shyness danced in her smile and her gaze dipped to his chest; a chest he puffed out a little under her examination.

"I guess this is a night of firsts for me."

"Me, too," he confessed, in part to comfort and part to calm his own racing heart.

"Oh?" Her voice didn't quite squeak, but her cheeks flushed when the higher note punched up the skepticism in the syllable.

He chuckled. "Absolutely. It's opening night. I've got a restaurant full of customers who came to sample the food, friends who made their reservations when I was still knocking down walls, and a crew of devoted employees who not only helped me choose the colors, but indulged every food experiment to help me pick out a menu." He rubbed his thumbs along the sides of her hands, seeking to soothe her rapid pulse.

Instead of responding to the intimacy of his confession, she withdrew. "I shouldn't have pulled you away from all of that."

Damon closed his hands around hers, keeping her turned toward him, and shook his head. "You didn't *pull* me away from anything. I am exactly where I want to be. The other firsts are dinner with a beautiful and charming woman whose deeply expressive nature reveals exactly what she thinks and feels about my food and my company, while doing me the incredible honor of sharing her birthday with me."

"Really?" The surprise widening her eyes couldn't be feigned, because like her response to the kiss and her nervousness, it reflected in the lean of her body away from him, the sudden rigid lift to her spine and the inescapable clench of her fingers against his palms.

"Absolutely. You came here tonight to meet someone." *Time for the frontal assault, no more games or misdirection.* He shifted his grip on her hands, sliding forward on his seat until his legs could brace the sides of her chair, effectively caging her in. *Just in case.*

"I know and I'm sorry he decided to miss out on the wonderful food, but I...."

"Wait. Please." She couldn't have slapped his conscience any harder if she'd tried. She was apologizing for being stood up and offering succor to his ego. He didn't deserve it. "You came here to meet someone, an arranged date through the 1Night Stand service."

Her beautiful, pouty lips whitened around the edges. He plowed forward, ready for the friendly fire.

"You weren't stood up. I came out with your coffee to introduce myself, and you assumed I was a waiter. I should have just corrected you, but you were so nervous and tired, that I decided to play along. Then you were simply beautiful in your responsiveness and I didn't want to make it awkward. Which is exactly what I'm doing now." He sighed and caressed the pulse points along her wrists with his thumbs. "I'm sorry for that. Truly sorry that I misled you. But I am not sorry that you're sitting in my restaurant, eating my food and sharing it with me, and I hope you'll find it in your heart to forgive this Marine."

"You're my date." She repeated the words, as though needing to say it aloud to make it real.

"Yes, ma'am."

She wasn't pulling away. That was a good sign. She wasn't slapping him and calling him a jerk. That was a better sign.

A laugh escaped on a breathy exhale and her gaze lifted to the wall behind him, before darting back as she processed the information. "I'm not sure why I assumed you were a waiter. I thought you were my date just playing along and then I thought I was wrong."

"I wasn't sure either. Most of the staff is in white shirts and slacks, although some of the women preferred skirts."

"You were too beautiful a man to be my date."

He let the beautiful comment skate by, but not the too part and lifted his brows, leaning his face in and letting his nose just brush hers. "That's an odd turn of phrase."

"Have you looked at you? Then looked at me?" The self-deprecation littering the question wasn't false either. She seemed to believe it.

He closed the distance between them and nipped her lower lip, pleased to see the color flood the white lines tightening the corners of her mouth. Resisting a smile, he gave her a stern frown. "First, I told you we don't speak badly of the ladies here, and I'd much rather look at you than myself, thank you very much. Second, you must have truly been dating the wrong men to think his looks are a barometer for whether he qualified to be your arm candy."

"Arm candy?" The sudden effusive laugh was exactly what he'd been hoping for. She rolled her eyes and shook her head. "No, I'm sorry, no man has ever qualified for my arm candy before...."

"So this makes me your first in that department. Very well. I accept and will do my best to live up to the title."

A red flush raced over her skin and her eyes glittered. He squeezed her hands lightly before retrieving their wine glasses and topping them off. Pressing her glass into her fingers, he clinked them together. "To a night of many firsts."

She hesitated and he read the quiet question in her eyes.

"Yes. I meant that exactly how you're thinking right now."

Her exhale was swift and she covered the little gasp of sound with a swallow of the wine while he hid a smile behind his own glass. Teasing a response from her would be the greatest pleasure of the night. He couldn't wait to see her eyes soft and dewy, hear the sweet, explosive breaths as he peeled away the layers of everyday armor to delve into the sensuous woman hiding behind the gray top and sensible skirt. He wanted to find the woman that chose the red-bottom shoes.

"Can I tell you a secret?" She took another swallow of liquid courage and he shifted toward her again, intrigued.

"Absolutely."

"I wanted you to be my date...even when I thought you were the waiter...."

"Wish granted." Their glasses clinked again. Her pink cheeks heightened the gleam in her eyes and he nodded toward the food. "Time to close your eyes."

"Oh...I forgot we were eating."

The chef in him winced—no one should forget his food, much less eating it. His masculine pride swelled. He'd made her forget the food.

She set the wine glass down and folded her hands in her lap. Her lashes lowered and he shifted his seat again, easing the ache of his too-swollen cock pressing against the cage of his pants. She was so damn responsive.

He'd begun the meal intending to feed her soul.

Now he intended to completely seduce her senses.

"The steak," he began, "Is a filet, cut thick to allow for a slower cook and richer juices...." When her tongue flicked out to moisten her lips, he forced himself to cut into the meat, but his body longed to thrust into hers, burying himself balls deep until little gasps were all she could make.

"...it's rubbed with extremely fine grinds of dark and light roasts and cooked slowly over open flame until the juices begin to flow."

Was it possible for the man to become even sexier? Her mouth watered at the description. Despite the meal she'd already consumed, the cheeses, the wine, the salad with its skirted steak soaked in sweet sin, and the creamy soup, her stomach still tingled in anticipation of what else he offered. The scrape of knife and fork against the plate sent awareness racing across her skin.

Her nipples ached against her normally comfortable bra, the fabric almost too much against the turgid little points. The dampness flooding her panties should embarrass the hell out of her, but all she could think about as she sat, eyes closed, waiting, was whether it was steak he'd offer, or another bliss-filled kiss.

A vague sensation of crazy danced through her mind. Things like this just didn't happen to her. She was the practical one. Legal briefs, takeout, and episodes of Grey's Anatomy populated her nights where the doctors spent more time on their love lives than their surgeries.

The rich scent of coffee teased her nostrils and her mouth opened. She expected the offering on the end of a fork, but his thumb caressed her lower lip as she took the bite from his fingertips. Curious, she caught his fingertip lightly with her teeth and lapped the flavor of the coffee-basted steak. The coiling tension in her middle exploded, sending languorous waves through her limbs and she sighed.

He tasted better than the food.

His chuckle sent her temperature climbing, but she didn't regret the action, releasing him with a half awkward kiss to his thumb before biting into the steak itself. A second wave of explosions rippled across her taste buds and she groaned.

Tender and juicy didn't do the flavor justice. The filet was warm, soft and seemed to break apart on her tongue. The rich meat flooded her senses, but riding the current above the marriage of blood, flame and smoke was the morning kiss of rich, gourmet coffee. The flavors tangled like a walkthrough between a Starbucks and a steakhouse. Her mind didn't know what to process first, but she swallowed the piece, torn between regret and anticipation, opening her mouth to ask for more only to find a second bite waiting for her.

He teased her with the last piece and let her draw on his fingers, chuckling as she lapped at the pads of his fingertips before devouring the bite. So they repeated the dance. He never failed to touch her, stroking her cheek, and even grazing her nose with his when he cleaned the dribbles that escaped with feather light kisses.

She fisted her hands, fighting the desire to reach out and

capture the scorching flame that engulfed her every time he came near. Tears gathered in the corners of her eyes and she barely felt the first trickle of dampness on her cheeks.

"Helena," his voice brooked no argument and her lashes lifted, tears falling freely. The trembling in her fingers seemed to vibrate through every bone until even her hair seemed to shiver from the assault on her senses. "What's wrong, sweetheart?"

The words wouldn't come. How could she explain the riots breaking out all over her body? Her breasts ached. Her wet sex clenched. Her toes curled insider her shoes. She shook with the force of the torrent racing through her blood. She tasted the food, but it was the flavor of *him* that lingered.

How could she explain how she never wanted these moments to end? How could words ever adequately describe the waves of emotion that swelled and dragged at her, tumbling over every practical objection her mind stuttered to produce?

He set aside the knife and fork. His hands cradling her cheeks as he brushed away the tears she couldn't even work up the embarrassment to hide as they slipped, one after another, out of her control.

"Tell me what you want, sweetheart," his voice trembled low and deep. The dark hair shaping his face was thick, barely long enough to graze the tops of his ears. His perfectly shaped ears, with their gentle whorls and lobes that looked ripe enough to graze with her teeth, to lap at with her tongue until he shivered.

His broad forehead crinkled with the frown drawing his dark brows together over his sensuously lit blue eyes. She'd called them bedroom eyes when she'd first glimpsed them, but they were so much more. They pushed past every barrier she erected, dodging her defenses or simply dismissing them. She wanted to drown in those eyes, sink into the sea of sumptuous pleasure they promised.

Swallowing past the lump filling her throat, she whispered, "You."

The admission cost her, it took every ounce of her strength to shape the word, nails digging into her palms as the quivers in her belly continued to ripple outwards, gaining in strength. The riptide of sensation jerked her under and she didn't want to fight it anymore.

"It would be my pleasure," he murmured. His mouth slanted over hers and robbed her of the need to say anything else. The world tilted and she surged forward, wrapping her arms and hopes around him, a tempest exploding within her as he lifted her out of the chair and into his lap.

Chapter Five

$\mathcal{D}$amon stroked his thumbs down her cheeks, urging her mouth to open wider for him. The silken heat of her bottom pressed against his raging hard on. He deepened the kiss. His tongue slid against the rough ridges of flesh behind her teeth and then up to tangle with hers. It was an altogether satisfying kiss, but he wanted more.

Her greedy little fingers fisted on his shirt. He nuzzled a trail of kisses from the corner of her mouth to taste the salty tears that continued to slip from her eyes. Raising his head, he waited for her lashes to flutter open, for the glistening warmth of her autumn brown eyes. Darker than wine, her pupils dilated as though the black sought to swallow up every last drop of light.

"When we built *Lagniappe's*, we added six apartments upstairs." He caressed one hand along the column of her throat to the silk of the gray blouse, smoothing the fabric over her shoulder until he reached the bare, warm flesh of her bicep. He wanted to touch every inch of her smooth skin.

She rolled her hips, her tight, round bottom rubbing the length of his erection, shredding his barely contained control.

Apprehension tensed her sweet, soft lips. He braced himself for her objections, her rejection. If she would spend the rest of her night sitting in his lap, he could get drunk off her hot, wet kisses and he would find a way to handle it.

"I'm not very good at it."

The confession reined in his raging libido and he tipped her chin up. Hints of shame clouded her damp, desire-filled eyes. Tears trembled on her lashes. Her chest rose and fell matching the ragged pant of her breaths.

"Not very good at what, sweetheart?" Because she was one hell of a responsive kisser, meeting him thrust for thrust, coaxing a wild heat in him that he was having a damn hard time keeping banked to even have the conversation. If not for the whisper of bodies beyond the privacy curtain, he'd lay her out on the table in front of him, peel up her skirt and feast on the sweet delicacy of her sex until he'd satisfied his craving to know every sound she could make.

His cock twitched, thoroughly encouraged by that game plan.

"Sex." The corner of her mouth turned down and her lashes dipped, hiding her eyes. "I tried it a few times in college."

He would not laugh, but the noise still escaped as a small snort. "Let me guess, fifteen minutes of fumbling in the dark, a few thrusts and he was done?"

God save him from frat boys more interested in firing the gun, than how to prime and prepare the field of engagement.

"More or less. It was awkward and it hurt and then it just...I really didn't get the fuss." She shifted, the awkward shyness bubbling up under the professional and extremely sexy woman. He dropped his hands to her hips, holding her still before he fired off a warning shot of his own.

"Sweetheart, I promise you extremely unpleasant college sex is the last thing I have in mind."

Red suffused her skin and her teeth grazed her lower lip. The absolute uncertainty was adorable and irritating in the same breath. "I thought you were asking me upstairs to...."

"Oh, I am definitely inviting you upstairs, and I plan to strip off every stitch of your clothing, lay you down on a bed, and explore every glorious inch of your flesh." He kept his gaze firmly on hers, rubbing her hips gently, a roaming caress that grazed up the side of her torso, then over her belly and down again to the thigh shrouded by her smart little skirt.

She really was wearing far too much clothing.

"The problem with college boys is they are too quick to shove their dick into any warm, wet orifice and forget that just because they're ready, their partner may not be."

The blush scalded her cheeks, but her lashes lifted, the provocative woman fighting to meet his gaze. "I don't want to be a disappointment...you've been amazing all evening...and I would hate to...."

He swallowed the rest of her words with a kiss. Bracing an arm beneath her, he pushed up from the chair and lifted her against him. Her arms wrapped around his neck and her chest plastered to his. He smiled, murmuring. "Yes or no, sweetheart. Then leave everything to me...."

"Yes." The word slid around his tongue as she dove back into the kiss. He barely managed to grab her purse strap with one hand before carrying her toward the red wall and nudging the latch that released the privacy door. He carried her down the quiet hallway and up the stairs to the private apartment. Behind him the door swished shut and locked. The door hidden by the paint job was a finishing touch he'd added when he realized how late or early he would want to be in the restaurant.

On the first landing, he gave her bottom a gentle tap. "Wrap your legs around me, sweetheart."

As she struggled to comply, he gave her skirt a little shove, freeing her legs. Her thighs tightened on his hips, and her ankles hooked over each other behind him, the tip of one heel tapping his thigh. The furnace of her sex pressed against his throbbing erection.

He pressed the key code for the electronic lock and released the door. Once inside, he dropped her purse nearby, but snagged the white silk scarf from the top. Then he strode through the darkened apartment, torturing himself by grinding against her heat with every step.

In the bedroom, he kicked the door shut and went to his knees at the bed as he sat her down, claiming her with another kiss. Her thighs spasmed, rocking her hips toward his invitingly.

He nibbled a path of kisses to her ear. "Do you have any attachment to this blouse?"

"No," she breathed. "I got it on sale at...."

He stopped listening at the no and gripped the lapels, ripping it open and sending the buttons bouncing across the wooden floors. Beneath the top, her breasts peeked at him from beneath cream-colored demi cups. Sweet, small and barely a palm full, he rubbed both of his hands over them.

The twin hard points of her nipples pressed against the scrap of cloth, but he continued the slow strokes, caressing her chest. He followed the dip into the valley between her breasts and along the edges of the bra until he rolled a slow, whorl around the stiffened flesh. His gaze never left her face and he smiled at her gasp of wonder.

"Sex is a lot like cooking." He rubbed one point between his thumb and forefinger. "You have to be patient. Some dishes are flash fried, hot and tempting, but others need loving care, spice rubs for example, need to be thoroughly massaged, ensuring a full flavor is absorbed by every ounce and then you lay it over the heat, and you cook it slowly until the juices flow...."

He leaned in, tugging one cup down and capturing the pebbled nipple, a whisper of pressure before teasing it with gentle laps. She fisted his hair, but he ignored the demand, taking his time to thoroughly sample the nipple, drawing it between his teeth until he could suck it properly. Her legs clenched against his hips. He traced a path with a single finger to the other cup and lavished the that nipple with the same treatment.

His cock ached with the urge to be free of its confinement, but he fought the need to rip off her panties and drive himself home. She wasn't ready, no matter how responsive her gasps and clenching fingers suggested. He pushed the blouse off her shoulders, and she let him go long enough to help him strip off the cloth in his way. Her bra followed and he paused to look at her.

Her breasts were pink and warm with the blush that crept from her face to stain the skin. She was slender, almost too slender. God he wanted to feed her until she filled out the promise of curves everywhere, but she was so perfect, with her pert, upturned breasts and rosy nipples straining toward him.

Roaming his hand over her abdomen, he smiled at the trembling muscles that flexed beneath his touch. Her skirt boasted a three-inch zipper over one hip. He tugged it down and gave her a gentle nudge, urging her to lay back. Peeling the skirt down, he eyed the lace shrouding her sex. She started to shake off a shoe and he caught the heel and pressed it back into place, meeting her gaze along the long line of her body.

"The shoes stay."

Her eyebrows lifted. He grinned and slid a finger under the edge of the lace to explore the dampness teasing his nostrils. The rich musk of her was a far more inviting aphrodisiac than the meal they'd shared earlier. Her thighs clamped on his hand, shoving him between the slick folds of her sex.

Working carefully up and down, he found her swollen clit and teased the treasured little nub with a gentle roll and laughed softly as her hips arched upward. Her eyes closed and her thighs spasmed on his wrist.

Another stroke of his finger and her body convulsed. Petting her through the orgasm, he could barely suppress a groan. If she could come apart with so little coaxing, what would she do when he went down on her?

Helena lost the capacity to think. Words fell away, unspoken, and all she felt seemed to center below her navel, a sweet suffocation of need stirring like a beast to storm through her body. Tingles turned to fireworks and she writhed against his hand, urging him closer and aching for more even as her body twisted with the tumult.

When he slid a finger inside of her, the muscles of her sex clenched against it and she wanted even more. Searing need speared her belly and she grabbed for the comforter, holding on lest she fly off into the ether. Desire tore apart her insides, shattering her completely.

"Let go, sweetheart," his words washed over her and another touch against her clit and she was lost.

Drifting back to herself, she felt rather than saw him move. Her panties glided down her legs, but he left her shoes in place. A silly little giggle bubbled out of her. Naughtiness threaded through her blood, and she pushed herself up on her elbows to watch as he shed his clothes. Jacket, shirt, and pants hit the chair she'd failed to notice in the corner. His cock curved up to his belly, the dark olive skin stretching and nearly reddened at the thick tip.

Her mouth watered as she took in the tight muscles of his thigh, the chiseled six pack of his abdomen and up to the broad plains of his chest with the sexy little curls of dark hair that beckoned her fingers to run through them, caressing the hard muscle. Nothing spare hung on him, he'd been carved like a Greek statue, but so much better.

Because he was all male, hard and hot.

Need bloomed in her belly, and she arched to meet his glide onto the bed, mouth open for another tongue-tying kiss. His hands were everywhere, caressing her, cradling her and teasing until she thought she'd come apart again. Acting on impulse, she mirrored his touches. She stroked her hands down his chest, exploring the flat nipples, delighting at their stiffening.

The heat of his cock rubbed against her thigh. He pulled away, and she watched in drowsy pleasure as he pulled out a condom. He rolled the latex into place and her mouth went dry. He was magnificently shaped and so huge. Trepidation weaved through her excitement.

"I don't know if you'll fit." Her heart thudded and she stifled another wave of nervous laughter at his unabashed grin.

He rolled over her, the hair on his chest teasing her nipples. He settled his raging erection against the nest of her sex. "Do you remember what I said downstairs?"

"Which part?" She fought the urge to lift her hips, the weight of him rubbed slowly against her, teasing her over sensitized clit until eddies of want drowned out the nervous thoughts bubbling to the surface.

"We don't talk badly about women. You are perfect. Perfect mouth." He kissed her, thrusting into her soul with his tongue as though to demonstrate. "Perfect breasts." His hand cupped her breast, massaging the nipple for emphasis. "And a perfect, responsive, hot, pussy."

He shifted the head of his cock, brushing her entrance and then he was pushing, in a long, slow stroke. He eased through the last of her defenses, stretching her sex until she thought she couldn't take any more and then he pushed deeper. His jaw tightened, a vein throbbing in his forehead as breath whistled through his teeth.

"So tight," he murmured before claiming her lips again, then his hips jerked forward and he was deeply seated inside of her. Her legs lifted of their own accord, and she wrapped them around his hips, allowing him greater access as he pulled back and thrust again.

The world narrowed to the motion of his cock and the tension of his mouth as the kisses took on a harder demand. He sucked her tongue and pursued it back into her mouth. The assault on her senses blotted out the world. She fought to hold onto some sense of herself. It was all skin sliding on skin, ripples of pleasure cascading from every point of contact and with every thrust, he grazed along her clit until the orgasm stormed through her and she could only dig her nails into his shoulders and hang on.

His shout followed hers and he bucked, his balls slapping her ass as he came. She forced her eyes open, drinking in the rapture twisting his expression until he collapsed into a pure masculine blanket of heat. Pleasure continued to eddy through her, drowning the shy reserve and she stroked the length of his spine, petting him as he'd caressed her earlier, and when her sex clenched around him, he groaned into her ear.

"Happy birthday, Helena."

God, he even made her name sound sexy.

ভ

He rolled over at the sound of the door and lifted his head. Dawn edged the windows, the sun already rousing to greet the morning. He didn't have to stretch out a hand to know she'd left. He'd taken her four times over the course of the night, indulging every idea that popped into his head.

At some point between lapping up the sweet cream of her desire and urging her to mount him, she'd murmured something about an early court appointment. It didn't allay the desire to reach over and take her again. Sighing, he shoved upward. He needed to check the restaurant. He'd abandoned his staff to handle the rest of opening night, enjoying the hell out of the wild woman she'd become in his bed and with dawn, their one-night stand over, he regretted not inviting her back.

Scrubbing a hand over his face, his gaze landed on the slender black rectangle that lay next to his pants on the chair and a lazy smile stretched across his face.

Her phone promised that she'd return.

He eyed the smart little device with satisfaction and started planning their next menu...

Her Marine

Heather Long

&

Chapter One

"So they've got us surrounded, good! Now we can fire in any direction, those bastards won't get away this time!"
– CHESTY PULLER, USMC

*B*rody checked the suit jacket's fit against his button down. He'd skipped the tie altogether. Dress blues were more comfortable than business slacks and a tie. Damon Sinclair leaned against the bedroom's doorframe. "If that doesn't fit, I can jog over to the Captain's or Logan's."

"Nah, it'll do." Brody stretched his arms. The jacket was snug, but not uncomfortable. "You're losing bulk."

Damon shrugged a shoulder. "I can still kick your ass. Sir." He tacked the last on as an afterthought.

Brody grinned. "You don't have to sir me."

"Old habits die after the Marine, not before him." Damon tossed him a set of keys. "I'm staying with Helena tonight, so the place is all yours."

"Thanks." Brody shoved the keys in his pocket. "Hey, Damon...is Matt okay?"

"He's fine. He has good days and he has bad days. Fortunately the good days are starting to beat the bad. Today's just not a good day. You stepping in for his date is a huge favor, one he'll appreciate. I think Doc and his lady are taking him out to dinner." Dinner with the Doc instead of his one-night stand might seem like a strange trade-off, but Brody didn't mind filling in or even being asked to fill in. A Marine needed his help, and that was all he required.

"Yeah, okay. It's not like getting laid is a hardship." Brody understood the younger Marine, Matt. The kid had found a home in the Corps. Brody never thought that having a family could make recovery worse, but then all he'd ever had to live up to was the Corps, and his brothers in the Marines.

"Tick tock, Lieutenant. You're gonna be late." Damon threw him a wave and was gone. The chef was in his element. Most of the guys were, with few exceptions. Even Logan seemed downright cheery when they went out for beers. The Captain was completely in love with his fiancée, the Doc was tight with an actress, and Logan couldn't shut up about a Gunnery Sergeant.

A Gunny.

Snorting, Brody inspected his appearance for neatness in the mirror and followed Damon out. The cook—sorry, chef—was already long gone. Apparently he'd met his match in an attorney, but it took a lot of patience on his part to keep her coming back for more. She must be worth it. He was damn near as cheery as Logan. The whole team seemed to be settling into civilian life.

Sliding into the driver's seat of the black hulk the guys loaned him for his leave, Brody couldn't begrudge any of them. He was one of the last of his unit still on active duty. The new guys were a decent crew, and he got along with them well enough, but it was still damn good to see the rest. Years of working together made the conversation easy, the jokes ribald, and the acceptance smooth. They didn't ask stupid questions, didn't mention things better left unsaid, and didn't give a good goddamn when they pissed him off.

The GPS turned on with the engine and Brody plugged in the club's address. Thirty-six hours earlier, he'd thrown his gear into the belly of a C-130 and left Germany for the long haul back to the States. Ten days of leave before he had to report in to the Navy

Yard in D.C. Ten days to grab some pick up games with the guys, play poker, drink beer, and give the Captain shit about his new, old lady.

Laughter rumbled in his chest. He checked the directions once before pulling out of the parking lot and leaving Mike's Place in the rearview mirror. Brody had known about Rebecca for years, he'd seen her name on the return address of many an envelope. It had been his job to isolate the notes and put them away for the Captain on more than one occasion. He was glad the two worked it out even if they'd met through some crazy sex service.

1Night Stand might be some exclusive outfit, but as far as he was concerned, they still hooked people up for sex. Not that he was complaining, it'd been more than a few months for him and the opportunity to spend the evening with some good-looking, willing woman didn't turn him off. Still, what kind of a woman signed up for something like that?

Apparently most of the women his friends were crazy for went for a one night stand, so maybe the service was on to something.

The drive from Allen to downtown Dallas took the better part of an hour with the thick traffic streaming into the city's nightclub scene. Brody checked his watch twice. The date was set for seven and the last thing he needed to be was late.

Shannon. Here's hoping she's not too pissed about being traded off to a different guy. But then, if she wants sex, well I got that covered.

He'd been a little suspicious initially about the call, until the Doc explained that Matt was just having a bad day and they'd already cleared it with the service.

Signing up for a date with the 1Night Stand service was a pact most of his boys made after they returned stateside. Some of the unit struggled with being back in the world. Matt was definitely one of them. To support their brothers in arms, most joined, even those who thought they couldn't possibly need it like Zach or Doc, or even the Captain. The success rate didn't ease his skepticism and while he was still in Iraq, he'd shrugged off joining. But he also gave his word that he'd do it when he stood down. Since he had no intentions of going off active until they carried his body off the field, he was set.

Traffic thinned as he swung the truck into the valet slip at the Sybarite Club. The sexy valet was a surprise, and he couldn't stop the grin when her perfectly rounded white globes threatened to burst out of the square corset. She palmed his keys and gave him a ticket, and a wink. Maybe if it didn't work out with *Shannon*, he could look this tall drink of water up.

The doorman was tall and evenly built, but his eyes were careful and assessing, his gaze scanning him quickly and efficiently. Brody liked him immediately. The doorman may be dressed for pomp and circumstance, but he served as protector and gatekeeper. Sliding the valet slip into his back pocket, he grabbed his wallet and flipped it to the black card with its silver lettering. Damon had dropped the private invite by with the dinner jacket.

"Welcome to the Sybarite Club, Lieutenant Essex." The topcoat and tails handed the card back and opened one of the dark cherry gothic style doors. The woodcuts might have startled him, but Doc had given him a heads up about the Sybarite's eclectic predilections. The door featured detailed cuts of a man and woman engaged in cunnilingus and fellatio. As the doors parted, each figure was left alone and crying out for the other.

Damn. Brody stared at the images for a heartbeat or three. The blatant sexuality both titillated and repulsed him. Sex should be hot, wet, primal, and not on public display. Head shaking, he skated a hand over his hair. He missed his cover and it felt odd to be without it.

On leave. The stern reminder didn't relax his shoulders or the tingle of anticipation shivering through his gut. Not quite marching inside, he followed the carpeted entryway down four steps into a dark lounge sparkling with a stage show of three women in lacy clothing and impossible positions, while a pulsing musical beat summoned images of tribal music through the blues with a hint of rock and roll.

Low lighting by way of paper lanterns sat on every table,

twisting long shadows from the dancers' performance. The women bumped, ground, and shimmied their hips in perfect synchronization. As his foot hit the last step, the three women froze, the lights dropped and a spotlight shone on a leggy redhead striding out from behind the curtains. If Jessica Rabbit was a real woman, she'd look like the singer who lifted the microphone to her lips and welcomed her audience with the low, husky whisper of an Italian Kathleen Turner.

That was sexier than the club doors.

The woman's voice perfumed the foreign lyrics with forbidden promises. Servers in unrelieved black slipped in and around the tables, delivering drinks and food without disturbing the spell woven on the stage. He didn't understand the woman's sultry Italian, but his lack didn't detract from the emotion.

Captivated, Brody stared as she massaged emotion from the music. His heart thudded a quiet counterpoint to the beat. Everything in the room hushed, from the whispers at the tables to the movement of the wait staff. When a man strolled out to meet the woman, she turned and caught his hand. He took up the song and it transformed from something provocative to a note that squeezed around his heart.

An echo of movement next to him tugged his gaze from the stage. A gorgeous woman stood next to him, her short black curls pinned carefully to frame her porcelain skin.

"They are singing about goodbye," she murmured, her voice almost too low to be heard over the voices twining together, lovers dancing around the notes of the man's baritone and the woman's husky alto.

"I don't know the words." He followed her lead, loathe to break the spell spinning between the two singers. Somewhere on the stage, dancers moved, but they were so understated, he doubted the crowd was quite aware of them.

"When I'm alone, I dream of the horizon and words fail me. There is no light in a room where there is no sun." The woman's words translated the underlying score of the singing. "And there is no sun if you're not here with me. From every window unfurls my heart, the heart you have won. Into me you've poured the light, this light you found by the side of the road."

Oddly, tears pricked the back of his eyes at the sweet little catch in the siren woman's voice. Pulling his gaze from the performers, he canted his head. Moisture glittered around the woman's impossibly long eyelashes, but while she watched the singers, one hand toyed with a coin hanging by a silver chain around her neck.

"She tells him it's time to say goodbye, places that I've never seen or experienced with you, now I shall. 'I'll sail with you upon ships across the seas, seas that will exist no more. It's time to say goodbye.'"

The music rose as the woman's voice faded. His siren's face arrested with emotion, her fingers white-knuckled around the coin.

On the stage, the man's voice rolled in, a gentle thunder promising a storm across the waves as the water whispered to the shore.

"He tells her, when she's far away, he dreams of the horizon and words fail him. He knows that she is with him, always with him. She is his moon, the sun, and no matter where he goes, she is with him, always and forever."

Brody didn't imagine the hint of tears sweeping through her words. He swallowed back the catch in his own throat. He'd witnessed too many goodbyes in the last decade, husbands, wives, or children wishing safety to their Marine as they headed overseas. He'd never envied those goodbyes, the poignant longing, the whispered promises, the quiet terror, or the brave faces. He never missed the letters carrying word of love and need, or the scratchy Skype calls with their glimpses of home.

Until now.

The siren paused as the music rose in crescendo and the man's baritone soared. "He tells her, it's time to say goodbye." She half swallowed the emotion around the last word. "Places that he has never seen or experienced with her, he will sail too, and carry her with him, across the seas, seas that will exist no more." A single tear slipped down her cheek, glistening in the flickering light as though illuminated by a morning sun.

"They are promising to revive them together, that they will be together on the seas, even though they are apart, that the sea will exist no more. She is with him and he with her, always." The final descant faded and the music ended, leaving only their haunting promise echoing in the air. The silence swelled and applause rippled across the room.

Brody applauded. His companion clapped as heartily, pausing only a moment to swipe away her tears. She grinned at him as the house lights came up, lightening the mood.

"Thank you." He meant the words.

"You're welcome."

He stared at her, the pert nose, high cheekbones, and the warm amber sea that made up her eyes, their color like a blend of soft tan and gold, an impossible shade. She was lean, tall, and willowy in a way that hinted at fragility. But her eyes were warm, strong, and nearly as haunting as the music she'd just translated. Even more impossible was the odd longing twisting his insides at the smile playing at the corners of her mouth.

"Brody Essex, ma'am." He found his manners somewhere and extended his hand. Her eyes widened a fraction as though in recognition and the smile dimmed a note.

"Shannon Fabray." His hand nearly engulfed hers. The chill in her fingers argued with the sultry heat of her eyes and he closed his fingers around hers, accepting the introduction, and wished he could warm them at the same time.

Shannon. My date?

"It's nice to meet you." He dragged the words out of the dusty confines of his social skills. "It's really damn nice to meet you."

Oh. Hell yes.

Chapter Two

Shannon looked up at the man holding her hand. The mild perplexity drawing his brows together when he listened to the music had drawn her like a moth to a flame. The performers offered a glimpse into the heady desire of a love that surpassed time and distance. She'd noticed Brody the moment he'd stepped into the club, sucking all the oxygen out of the room with him. Years spent studying the masculine form didn't prepare her for the absolute maleness of him.

His cream-colored button down glowed faintly under the muted light. With the addition of a dark suit jacket and comfortable jeans, he screamed raw sexuality. His chiseled face, honed down to the bare masculine essentials. Strong cheekbones descended into a squared jaw with just the hint of roundness to blunt the edge. Clean-shaven, his face was tanned copper suggesting hours in the sun. He wore his dark hair cropped in a standard, high and tight Marine cut with the edges buzzed above his ears.

Even the man's ears were shaped well, perfect whorls close to his head with a seductively curved arch. Her palms itched as she studied his profile. Sculpting him would take hours. Subtle shifts in his expression suggested far more complex emotions than were readily visible at first glance. His rounded eyes had just the barest hint of a tilt to the edges. Lines of tension webbed out from their corners. He held himself erect, shoulders back, yet despite the stiff appearance of his posture, he stood before her, relaxed.

She read it in every even line of his body.

Stripping him mentally, she wanted to study the lines of his musculature. Would his chest dimple at the center over his sternum? Would his waist narrow below his ribs? Would he have thick, evenly spaced, washboard abdominals? Would his hips flare, hardening with tension where the skin stretched over his ass and down his thighs?

Moisture gathered in her panties and she forced her gaze upward. She was there to meet the man, maybe sleep with him, not strip him naked to sculpt him.

But damn if she didn't want the chance to at least run her fingers over the shapes.

"It's nice to meet you." Brody dragged the words out slowly. "It's really damn nice to meet you."

His voice carried just the vaguest hint of a New England accent, with hard vowels easing into the slow roll of his consonants. The way he spoke was both exotic and provocative.

"It's nice to meet you, too." An entire hive of bees bounced around in her stomach, teasing the anxiety humming in her blood, and sending chill-laced tingles dancing over her skin. *This is why I'm here. The big, brilliant plan to get over the fear of being touched. God, does he have to keep holding my hand?*

She fought the urge to jerk her fingers free as the moments he held her hand threatened to lengthen. Not fidgeting was harder than she ever imagined. Thankfully, a waitress chose that moment to glide up to them. Brody's mouth quirked into a small smile for the woman, but he barely looked at her.

"Lieutenant Essex, Miss Fabray, your table is ready."

Lieutenant. Like a light bulb swinging on a solitary chain, the accent, the dress and even his posture made so much more sense. He was military. Likely active military if the waitress wasn't calling him mister.

Sucking her lower lip, Shannon tasted the chocolate raspberry lip-gloss she'd decorated her mouth with as an afterthought. She hated make up and rarely bothered to mess with her hair. If Jeanine hadn't insisted on coming over to the studio before her date, she'd probably have shown up in jeans, a T-shirt and her hair in a ponytail. As it was, the deep purple slacks and blousy black top with ties gathered snug around her too small breasts offered a different illusion. Her black velvet ballet flats skipped the need to balance ridiculously on heels altogether. She spent too many hours of her day barefoot to try and torture herself in heels.

"Shall we?" Brody's voice nudged her out of her ruminations and a guilty flush heated up the chill on her skin. She stood, staring at him.

Nodding, she finally dragged her gaze away and followed after the waitress. Brody closed the gap behind her, the warmth of him teasing her spine as they weaved around the crowded room to a small table tucked comfortably against the wall. The high-backed booth gave them a suggestion of privacy, but they could still see the stage.

Brody waited until she was seated, giving her a long considering look before sliding into the opposite side of the booth. She'd sat near the edge, not allowing him any room to join her on her side of the half round. Should she have scooted over?

Indecision tangled with self-preservation. She'd shaken his hand, which was a solid first step. Maybe waiting before he touched her again was a good idea. But even as that thought cemented in her mind, his leg brushed hers beneath the table.

She froze. The hard length of male calf seemed to burn right through the layers of clothing separating them. The heat seeped in, chasing the chill, and sent an entirely different wave of tingles dancing across her nerve endings.

"Would you like something to drink? Or to hear about the specials?"

"I'll take a beer, whatever you have on draft is fine." Brody's words may have been aimed at the waitress, but his gaze locked on Shannon's and a wrinkle of worry formed between his brows.

Alcohol right now would be a bad idea. Her insides shredded, torn between the desire to bolt and the desire to touch. *Stop it. He hasn't done anything to threaten you or make you feel bad. Just order a damn drink already.*

"Actually, could I get a latte? With cinnamon?"

If Brody was surprised by her order, he didn't show it. The waitress nodded, but she kept looking at him anyway. The waitress moistened her lips. The woman's blatant interest annoyed Shannon. But he hadn't looked up or taken his eyes off of her.

"Are you all right?" His voice sent all kinds of shivery prickles through her.

"No. Yes. Um...." Mortification punched through the words. Heat swept up her cheeks and she clenched her hands on the table to keep from covering her face with them.

"Can I take D, all of the above then?" Compassion eased the words, but his gaze never wavered nor lost its sober, serious gleam.

"I'm sorry, I'm not usually this batty." God, she should go in the bathroom and smack herself. The man sitting across from her was gorgeous. But it wasn't just the contours of his face or the lines of experience etched into his features. He was just so male, everything about him humming with masculinity from the spicy musk of his scent to the hard lips that gentled into a smile.

"Batty?" Laughter breathed under the word. "I don't think I've heard that since one of the nuns yelled at me for driving her batty by canoodling with the girls."

"It's a word." Shannon shifted her weight and clenched her butt cheeks, fighting the urge to fidget. The warring sensations in her body sharpened the dampness soaking her panties. The visceral physical reaction seemed to be completely at odds with the nervousness tap dancing on her heart. "It's got character and it sort of sums up how I'm feeling."

He waited a beat as the waitress delivered their drinks. The lights reflected through his golden beer and shimmered against the crown of thick foam at the top of the icy mug, while her coffee steamed and added a hint of cinnamon and pumpkin to the air around them. He held up a hand to the waitress, silencing the woman before she could speak. "Can you bring us a sampler platter of some kind, and give us a bit?"

The waitress murmured an 'of course' and disappeared again. Wrapping her too cold fingers around the bowl shaped coffee cup, Shannon suppressed a shiver.

"All right, who was he and do you need his legs broken?" The comfort with easy brutality he offered didn't detract from the concern in his face or the targeted assessment in his eyes.

"I'm sorry." She blurted and ducked her head. The entire exercise was a terrible idea. Who was she kidding? She couldn't spend five minutes with a real man without coming apart at the seams, much less bed one or rediscover the passion missing in her work.

"Hey, you've got nothing to be sorry about. I'm a total stranger, but someone hurt you and I'm guessing it was a guy. So if you want his legs broken, I can buy you dinner, take care of that, and drive you home."

"You're serious?" She glanced up at him through her bangs, afraid to meet his eyes.

"Absolutely. Only a chickenshit bastard hurts a lady. I have no patience for that. So you tell me about him, we eat, and I'll take care of it."

Was he for real? Shannon couldn't quite wrap her mind around the dead serious offer. Nothing in Brody's demeanor suggested a joke or even a line. His gaze remained calm, intense, and focused on her. He didn't pay any attention to the scantily clad women on the stage demonstrating their flexibility. She squirmed under the brunt of his stare.

"You didn't show up for this date to get into a fight."

"A fight requires someone hitting me back. Trust me." Brody grinned—a long, slow grin that wrapped around her heart and tugged it away from punching her ribs. "He won't. And if he does, that will just make it more fun."

The laugh escaped before she could swallow it. Her lips trembled and she smiled. "I think that's the most romantic thing anyone's ever said to me."

"Then you have been seeing the wrong men, ma'am." Brody paused as the waitress brought a platter of fried foods, potato skins, mozzarella sticks, chicken wings, and more. Shannon's stomach let loose with a gurgle of hunger as the scents assaulted her. He waved the waitress off and set a small plate in front of her. "Ladies, first."

"Lieutenant Essex...."

"Brody."

"Brody, I can't believe I'm saying this, but I think tonight was a mistake." She fought the urge to reach for the food, twisting her icy fingers around the coffee cup, desperate for the heat.

"Maybe. But it wouldn't be the first one I've ever made, and the food is good, the music is pretty nice, and you've got a great smile. So let's eat." He shoved the platter at her. "What was the son-of-a-bitch's name?"

Shannon reached for the platter obediently but hesitated as her fingers grazed the edge of the fried cheese. "I don't know his name."

Brody nudged the plate again and she picked up the cheesy appetizer. Dipping it once into marinara sauce, she lifted and ate it. Aware of his approving gaze, she chewed thoughtfully.

"Good?" He spun the plate until the sticks faced him and the potato skins were closer to her.

Everything smelled good. It was all terrifically bad for her, but her stomach didn't give a damn about nutritional value. Finished with her first selection, she picked up a potato skin and two barbecue wings to add to her plate. She couldn't help another smile at his nod.

"Yes. I am such a mess."

"You're hungry and you're nervous, and I'm a complete stranger. But that has its benefits, too."

He was just so damn matter-of-fact. He picked up one of the barbecue wings and ate his way through it with absolute neatness. She watched his lips move against the saucy skin. They were firm, determined, and sumptuous. Especially when his tongue flicked out to lick his lips. Her calf relaxed fractionally as his leg leaned on hers. Or maybe her leg was leaning against his.

"Besides looking at a living piece of art, I'm not sure what the benefits are."

He stared pointedly at her plate and she let out a little huff then picked up the potato skin, nibbling the edge until the flavors of crisp potato, melted cheese and bacon caressed her tongue.

"You can say anything you want, I'm not going to judge. You don't have to see me tomorrow. There's a lot of freedom when it's only about tonight."

"But you came here for sex." She said the word "sex" a lot louder than she intended as the music chose that moment to dip into a low note. Heat filled her face and she covered her mouth.

His soft laughter stroked her from across the table. "I came here to meet a beautiful woman, listen to some sweet music, and eat dinner."

"I guess two out of three isn't bad."

"This can be dinner, it all depends on what you're in the mood for." His mouth quirked and she heard the gentle rebuke. He wasn't letting her get away with dismissing her own looks. But she knew she was far from glamorous like the women on stage, or as provocative as the women dining around him. Heck, the waitress looked more seductive than she did.

Why hadn't she worn a dress? Or something more attractive?

"You're too nice."

He shrugged. "I don't have time for pretty words or empty compliments." He added more food to her little plate before wiping his fingers on a napkin and taking a drink of his beer. "Do you want something else to go with this? Steak? Chicken? Fish?"

"What is it with you and food?"

"You're nervous. Which means you probably didn't eat much today. You're cold. Which means your system is crashing. You're sweet. Which means you are sitting there feeling bad about not being something else instead of just relaxing and being who you are. Food can help with two of those and we'll work on the rest. Now, eat." The conviction and honesty in his words laid her soul bare and she reacted to the order.

Again.

She picked up a barbecue wing with both hands and turned it around in her fingers before taking a bite. Brody was right. He was a stranger. He'd come there, vetted by 1Night Stand, just like she had been. He wasn't a crazy or a psychotic. He was beyond kind, orders notwithstanding. But she didn't even reject the command in his tone, if anything it just made him sexier.

"I was raped." She admitted this to the chicken wing, careful not to look at him. "I don't remember it. I don't remember him. I don't even remember who it could have been." The words slid out of the rusty vault on a hint of tears, but she blinked them back. Five years of therapy might finally pay off. "I was at a party and then I woke up, in my own dorm room, naked, used, and bruised. No one saw me leave with anyone, and no one reported anything amiss. It took me three days to even call it in and by then it was too late. What evidence they could gather was never enough."

Putting the chicken wing down, she dared a look at Brody. His expression remained steady but there was a fierce edge to the air around him. "I don't know who he is or why he did it or if it really was rape. Maybe I consented. But I just never got past it. I did therapy, I changed schools, I threw myself into my work and here I am trying to look at a guy and not wonder if I'll wake up tomorrow and not remember any of it."

The whole idea was ridiculous. Critics called her work cold, divorced of emotion, and empty of passion no matter how clinically beautiful. She thought if she could get past her hang-ups, she could find that passion they said was so sorely lacking. She thought the service offered by the 1Night Stand would be perfect.

Safe, sexy, and simple.

Her stomach twisted around the food she'd eaten. Dropping the remnants in her fingers on the plate, she leaned back. "And before you say anything, I won't be offended if you want to bail. I thought I was ready for this and now I'm not so sure."

"You don't know me, Shannon, so I'm going to forgive that

insult to my honor. *I* would be offended if I walked away, so please don't suggest it again. Whether anything else happens tonight or not, I'm having dinner with the sexiest woman I've seen in a long time. She's smart, she speaks Italian, and I really need her to stick around."

"Why?" She couldn't help but ask the question.

Brody gestured to the stage. "They're going to sing again, and I'm not really going to understand it if I don't speak the language."

She twisted to see the couple strolling onto the stage while the house lights dimmed and the stretched-too-thin feeling warping everything inside of her relaxed. Slow, sensuous piano notes drifted across the hushed whispering through the club. Brody's leg abandoned hers and a soft swishing pulled her attention back to him. He'd slid over in the booth and when his gaze caught hers, he tapped the spot next to him. Her heart pounded. Terror and excitement engaged each other in a fierce tug of war.

The singer's low, husky voice sang in the sultriest notes. Shannon could stay safely where she was, and keep her distance. Or she could gather up the dregs of her courage and swap to the other side of the table.

Brody said nothing, merely watching her as the woman sang of the approaching night. If she sat there and remained a coward, he wouldn't think any less of her. It didn't matter that they'd just met and barely spent an hour together. She'd read it clearly in his even expression. He was on board with anything she wanted to do.

The hell with it....

Pushing her cup away carefully, she slid out of the booth and joined him before she changed her mind. The seat was warm from his body and the heat bolstered her flagging confidence. Brody smiled as he edged forward a bare fraction and murmured, "Tell me what they're singing about."

The whisper of his breath tickled her ear and she looked away from the singers to find his face just inches from her own.

Dear God, he's even more beautiful up close...

Chapter Three

*B*rody braced one arm against the back of the booth, not quite allowing it to touch her. Everything about her screamed fragility, but a core of strength lay beneath her fragile exterior. The quaver in her voice when she confessed why she'd come on this 1Night Stand shamed his earlier thoughts. Thankfully, he'd never voiced them so he had no apologies to make. He could wish she knew who had assaulted her. Breaking a man's legs was easier than destroying a ghost.

"I am guessing this is a play in several parts because they are singing of seeing each other the first time and their first meeting." Shannon shifted toward him, her voice pitched low.

He remained completely still. He'd met enough girls in foster care, girls who'd been abused, girls who'd been molested, and more than one who fell in with the wrong boyfriend and perpetuated that cycle. It took strength to act. It took more strength not to react.

"It was a dark day, she was so alone, not a friend to lean on, and then he came. He brought the sun with him, chasing away all the dark shadows in her life. She did not learn to breathe until he was there."

The little catch in her throat was back. The emotion quivering in her shivery tones beckoned to him. He'd never been one to walk away, not even from the most damaged of situations. He'd protected his fair share of strays through the years and every instinct screamed to protect this one.

"He remembers the day as she does, the clouds on the face of the moon, the stars blotted out, with only heaven's tears to bathe in and then she walked in and the sun tumbled from the skies to walk along the road, warming his path and bringing him home."

Brody spared the singers a glance. The pair stood at opposite ends of the stage, their backs to each other. The gulf between them was as palpable in the music, their song, and in Shannon's voice.

"She wants to always walk in the sun, but knows that even the brightest of days must give away to night and though they had to say goodbye, she carries the sunshine in her breast and will nurture it there." A low sigh escaped on the last word, but the man's voice picked up the descant and carried the song.

Despite the Italian and the soaring strength of his voice, he sounded nothing like the woman he romanced in song. His words were blunted, climbing one above the other in anger, worry, and need.

"When the evening falls, and the daylight fades, he hears her calling within him. He wonders if he is sleeping and that thought pulls him away, but then she is there and it holds him completely, keeping him close though he is so far away." Absorbed by the music, Shannon relaxed and her shoulder brushed his chest, lightly at first, but when she turned to continue translating the slender weight of her pressed against his side.

"She is alone as she walks into the room, the shadows around her, but from another world, where no other can follow, she hears him call to her. She follows him in her dreams, where she can cross over, never feeling close to home when he is so far away. In her dreams, he is searching, forever lost, forever hoping, clinging to the driftwood of memories, memories that tie them together." Her slender fingers curled into a fist and Brody studied the whitening knuckles. Letting go of his beer glass, he reached over and laid his hand over hers. Her soft, sharp inhalation pressed her closer to him. But he forced his fingers to relax, to drape over her hand as though a cloak, a human shield against the sadness ebbing in the song.

Her breath escaped in a whispery hiss, but she neither pulled away nor stiffened further. As the man took up the song again, she might have even relaxed. Or maybe it was Brody's imagination.

"He knows he will be waking soon and she will not be there when he opens his eyes, and though he is leaving, he must try to go on believing that their time together in dreams is real. He doesn't know the reason, but it is as close as he can come to home across that ocean of reason. He will hold fast to it and he will find his way to her again." She went silent, the music rolling over the man's last note and then the stage went black. The applause, when it came, cracked like multiple gunshots through the reverent silence.

Shannon jerked and Brody wrapped his arm around her. "It's okay," he murmured and her shaky laugh relaxed the tension in her shoulders. Squeezing her once, he loosened his hold so she could shift away if she chose.

As the lights came up and jugglers bounced onto the stage to lighten the gloom created by the singers, she dared a look at him. He met the nervous gaze with an easy smile. "You're really quite good at that translating."

"Thank you. I did an exchange program in Florence when I was in high school."

"I've never made it to Italy. I'll have to go now."

"I loved it. I always said I would go back, but I've never had the time or the money." A flush stole over her face. "What is it about you? I just keep saying the first thing in my mind. I'm usually a lot more filtered than this."

"I like this. So don't change. What did you love most about Italy?" He glanced up and caught the waitress's eye. With a jerk of his chin, Brody nodded to the coffee cup and held up two fingers.

"The art, the history, the feeling of walking down the same roads that the Medici's traveled, where the riots happened, where some of the greatest artists came to study, and the greater artists built their magnificent monuments. It was home to Michelangelo, del Verrocchio and so many others. The Renaissance was born there. I didn't think I would ever get tired of the city, and my host family was wonderful. They took me to see everything, willing to spend hours as I sketched, and studied." The wild light in her eyes transformed her from simply lovely to absolutely stunning.

"You're an artist."

The blush rising in her cheeks added another facet of loveliness. "Guilty."

"What kind of art do you do?"

Shannon hesitated as the waitress brought over two fresh cups of the cinnamon coffee. Brody slid her hand over to the cup and gave her a light squeeze before staging a strategic withdrawal. She was still sitting right next to him, her leg pressed against his, her shoulder leaning against his chest and his arm around her back where his fingers could just toy with the collar of her jacket.

He could stand to let go of her hand.

"I'm a sculptor and it sounds a lot more glamorous than it is."

"I don't know." He cocked his head and looked at her with a smile. "I think you're pretty glamorous."

She paused, coffee cup halfway to her lips, and burst out laughing. It was the first real laugh he'd heard fall from her lips since he'd arrived at the club. It was rich, throaty, and filled with life. The laughter created sparks in her amber eyes, heating them as though a candle flickered just behind the irises. The sound reached inside of him and gathered his guts up in a fist, shaking him to the core.

"I've been called a lot of things. But never glamorous." She set down the coffee cup and twisted toward him. Her thigh slid along the seat until her knee tucked up. The casual contact sent a flood of heat into his stirring cock.

"Do these look like glamorous hands to you?" Shannon held up her fingers. Slender and evenly shaped, they boasted little to no nail length. Her knuckles were scraped, every single one, and the skin was torn, red and fleshy along the edges. Frowning, he caught her offered wrists, turning her hands out so he could inspect the callused palms.

"No. They look like strong, capable hands unafraid of getting dirty, doing hard work, or reaching out to grasp what they want." They looked like the hands of any Marine after weeks in the desert—parched fingers, cracked and blistered from the heat, and cut and scraped from the work.

Her eye twitched and Brody lifted her hands to his lips where he could lay a kiss to the tips of each hand. "A lot like the very smart, sexy woman in front of me."

"How do you do that?" Her eyes widened a little, but her smile dazzled.

"Do what?" His brows rose in quiet challenge.

"Turn a negative into such a positive. I can't possibly be what you imagined for tonight."

"I work with what I have and when you spend your life with very little, you learn to appreciate every nuance of what is there as opposed to what might be. I had no illusions about tonight, so please stop picturing me as some brute who just wants to take you out to his car for a quickie in the back seat. I don't have time for beggars or bullshit. I like you. You're funny. You're smart. You're sexy. You don't eat a lot." The corner of his mouth quirked up at her second burst of laughter.

"I like you, too." The words bounced with the weight of her smile. "I thought it was ridiculous to sign up for a one-night stand...."

Brody lowered her hands, holding them lightly. He enjoyed the fact that she didn't pull away. "Why did you sign up?"

"I don't want to be a downer."

"Honesty isn't a downer. If you don't want to tell me, that's fine. But I would like to know."

He didn't push, but he also didn't pull his gaze away, not even for the crazy carnival characters laughing and dancing on the stage. The room faded behind her, a blurred background where the only sharply defined image was her sweetheart face creased by indecision.

"I make men." Her lips twisted as though she thought better of the statement, so Brody waited for it to play out. "I make sculptures of men. It's what I specialize in. I love the male body, the shape, the contours, the strength, the rugged and the soft. I love every part of it. But ever since college, one teacher after another, one art critic after another, has said my work is too cold, too clinical and it lacks passion." She nibbled on her lower lip.

"So you want to capture the passion again?"

"Yes. I don't date. I don't like men, I mean I like guys, a lot of them, but only as friends." She sighed. "This keeps coming out wrong."

"You're scared." Brody tested a theory and raised his hand to stroke a finger down her cheek. She went completely still at the action, but she didn't withdraw. Her pupils dilated, her lips parted, and her breathing grew shallow. "You're really scared, and you're not even sure totally what you're scared of. That makes it harder to put into words."

He paid attention to the sensitivity training he'd received. As an officer, it was his job to look after his men and to watch for the warning signs. Posttraumatic stress radiated off Shannon, whether she was aware of it or not and made worse because she didn't remember her assault, just the guilt and shame of waking up after the fact.

"It seems easier with you. Maybe you're right, it's because you're a stranger, but you don't even feel like a stranger now."

He liked that admission and continued to stroke her cheek gently. She relaxed. Brody was a patient guy and he could give her the time she needed. "I have an idea...it's a little unconventional though."

"Oh?" Interest flared in her eyes.

"I take it you have a studio?"

"Yes. A loft space in a always a marine warehouse."

"How far away is it?" He traced the line of her jaw, edging gently toward her ear and down again to her chin, the motion smooth and even.

"Just a couple of blocks, actually. A huge section of this area used to be nothing but old industrial warehouses. But most are converted lofts, apartments, studios, and clubs."

He slowly nodded. "Would you be comfortable taking me

there?"

Her breath caught and her chin jerked up. "Why?"

"You want to touch, to find the passion for the body again. I happen to have a body, and you can touch me at your leisure with no expectations, no demands, and all the control you could desire."

When she pulled back, he released her and let his hand rest on the back of the booth. Her mouth worked, but no sound emerged. A wild battle waged inside of her and every emotion flickered across her expressive face. Brody ordered himself to still and gentled his expression. It was a crazy idea, but fear was an insidious enemy. It burrowed in, sinking hooks into the tender part of the soul, rending and tearing when it was tugged at. Soon it became easier to hold onto the fear than risk the wounds of breaking free.

He understood it.

He'd fought it every day in Afghanistan, Iraq, Somalia and more countries than he could name. He fought it when he got on a plane, when he stepped out of a Humvee and when he woke up in the morning. He never let the hooks sink in. She wanted to rip them out. It was why she'd signed up with the 1Night Stand service. She wanted to find passion with a stranger, face down her fears and drive them away.

Brody was the right guy for the job. He'd face down every fear, no matter how bad it left him aching.

"I don't know if I can," she admitted.

"But you want to try." He heard her unspoken words.

At her slow nod, he slipped his hand around the back of her neck in a light caress. Her pulse beat madly in her throat. "Nothing will happen that you don't want to happen. You want it to stop, you say stop. You want me to hush, say hush. You say it and I will do it, you have my word."

"Do you mind if we walk there? It's not far and the crime rate's really dropped in this area."

"Sweetheart, it would be my honor to walk you to your studio, and trust me, no one is going to bother you."

Chapter Four

*S*hannon folded her arms across her chest as they stepped outside the club. The October air carried the promise of chill, but warmth from the day still drifted up from the cement. The smell of car exhaust mingled with scents of ivy, a hint of beer and from upwind, the rich, roasting aroma of beef from the steakhouse a block away. Brody spoke to the valet and came back with his keys. He wanted access to his car in case the club closed before he returned. He walked with such an easy, loping confidence. His posture never varied and his shoulders never slumped.

He really was a beautiful man.

And she was completely out of her mind. He lifted his brows at her.

"Oh." Another blush rushed to her cheeks. She'd forgotten he didn't know which way, and she pointed east up the block. "It's this way."

He hooked his thumbs into his jean pockets and cocked an elbow toward her. Uncrossing her arms, she slid her hand carefully into the nook created. He tugged her a fraction closer, sandwiching her hand into the warm of his body.

"Are you for real?" When she'd signed up for the one-night stand, she'd read all the literature, forced herself through the online interviews and questionnaires with the idea that it would all be worth it, if she could just get back on that horse again, take control of her reactions, and her body.

"Last time I checked. Want to pinch me and find out?"

"No." She shook her head, laughing at herself. "If I am imagining all of this, I don't want to wake up." The words sang with more truth than she could have believed. A surreptitious glance at her watch told her it had been less than two hours since she'd walked up to Brody in the club, since she translated that first song and been transported by the sweeping emotions in the words to this warm bubble that now included the Marine.

Sitting in the booth, she'd forgotten how tall he was. He stood more than a head taller than her, the perfect height to rest her head on his shoulder. It helped that he shortened his stride to accommodate hers and once again she was grateful not to be teetering on high heels.

"If you were imagining all this, what would you change?"

"Hmm...I'd be taller, prettier and a heck of a lot more confident." The words rolled off her tongue without a second thought, but they trembled with honesty. An honesty that was easier with Brody than any person she'd ever met. "Do you believe in reincarnation?"

He didn't answer immediately. At the corner, he leaned away to hit the button and waited for the walk signal before answering. "I don't *not* believe in it, but I can't say I've really thought about it that much, either. Why?"

She twisted to walk sideways, wanting to see his face, but her hand stayed firm in his arm. The casual contact was almost overwhelming in its intimacy. "Because I've known you for less than two hours and you're easy to talk to. I never thought anyone in the military would be easy to talk to, so damn easy to look at, or that I would invite him back to my studio."

Amusement crinkled the corners of his eyes. "And you've known a lot of us 'military' types?"

"A couple. Army mostly."

"Oh. *Them.* That explains it. You just needed to meet a Marine, ma'am." The easy wink and gentle smile boosted her hear, and she skipped a half step and then they were at her building. Her legs locked, as though the cement reached up to grab her ankles.

Indecision swept over her. What was she doing, inviting him back to her place? Had she invited him? Or had he invited himself? Raw terror clawed at the insides of her belly and scraped against her spine.

What if she couldn't go through with it? Was that fair to him? Wouldn't that make her a tease of the worse kind?

"You're having a whole conversation inside that beautiful head." Brody's slow drawl tugged her gaze upward. He tilted his head, consideration and patience tangible in his gentle smile. "Be nice if you'd invite a guy to participate in his own defense."

"I'm crazy," she blurted.

"Okay."

"What?" Shannon blinked, turning until she faced him. He shifted his arm, her grip slid off the crook of his elbow, but he caught her hand in his. The chill of the air teased the warmth suffusing her hand, adding tingles to where his fingers caressed hers.

"Okay, you're crazy."

"How is that okay?"

"Because crazy is in the eye of the beholder. I've jumped out of planes, driven right into enemy fire, and conducted building-by-building searches in hostile territory for insurgents where the natives would be just as happy to blow my head off. Top that."

Shannon's mouth opened and then promptly closed. Her heart pumped a little drum cadence against her ribs. Laughter popped the bubbles of nervousness flooding through her. "Are you sure you want to come up to the studio?"

"Only if you want me there. Remember, this is all about you. You control what we do and you make the decisions. I am in your hands, ma'am."

Absolutely no artifice, teasing, or even hint of untruth flavored the words. The earnest declaration carried simple fait accompli. He meant it. Her confidence unraveled swifter than she could gather it together.

Get it together, Shannon. This is what you wanted. To feel, to touch, to look, and to experience passion again. Passion is standing right there, staring at you with those fuck-me-hard brown eyes and love-me-longer lips.

"All right." Nothing like grabbing the bull by the horns. Or the Marine by the hand. She squeezed his fingers lightly. "We go upstairs, I can show you around the studio, and we take it slow."

"Yes, ma'am." The verbal snap of his heels in his words emboldened her further.

"But if I say no...."

"No means no, ma'am."

She giggled. "Please don't call me, ma'am."

His eyes crinkled with amusement. "Sir, yes sir."

Laughter burst through her nerves, and she shook with it as she plucked her keys from a pocket and let him into the building.

‍ᘓ

They rode up the rickety basket elevator to the top floor, and Brody waited patiently while she disengaged the electronic security and relocked the door's four slide bolts. Shannon leased the entire top floor of the converted warehouse, with statues and sculptures in various states of completion filling a full half. She'd been getting ready for another show and she'd already sold three of her marbles. Their owners loaned them back to her for the duration of the show. But the dispassion her critics pointed out was easy to see in the warm yellow light of the studio's night system.

Her heart started jogging as she watched him stroll through the studio space. His gaze seemed to absorb every inch of the vaulted ceilings, the floor to ceiling windows, the stone and wooden bracers that created an illusion of filler, and the statues themselves. Brody paused in front of one, a sandstone-colored marble of a man sitting with a laptop propped open on his lap. Modeled on Rodin's, The Thinker, she'd added careful hints of modern technology from the computer to the iPhone sticking out of one pocket. The phone had taken her a week to get right.

"Where do you want me?" He stood in the center of the room, patient and relaxed.

"You are so male." Her breath caught in her throat as she stared at him. In the low illumination of the studio's nightlights he was pure man, shadows feathered half his face, casting him in sharp relief. His lips were barely parted, but were full, firm and even. His nose curved gently along the line of his profile, adding just the barest hint of softness to the hard jaw line.

"Thank you." The easy grin stretched his mouth wide, but she shook her head slowly.

"Don't smile and just stay right there." She stripped off her jacket and tossed it uncaringly onto a table littered with brushes, pencils, sketch pads and chisels. She fumbled through the stack until she found a clean sketchpad and a pencil.

Sliding off her shoes, she padded in a circle around him. The light was damn near perfect, but with only a look over her shoulder at him, she bounced over to the wall switches. Flicking two off, she glanced back and grinned. The change bathed him in a pale, golden glow and gave his tanned skin a burnished edge. The shadows were softer.

He watched her with amusement glittering in his gaze, but his lips were relaxed and unsmiling, just like she'd said.

Now to find the perfect spot....

Somewhere between deciding on the settings and where to sit, her heart calmed to a gentle, sure cadence. The tension eased out of her joints and she moved in a slow loose, fashion. Brody waited patiently until she'd settled, six feet away from him. Gliding down into a yoga position, she hooked her ankles on her knees and flipped open the sketchpad.

"How long can you stand like that?" she asked, her chin tilted up and pencil poised.

"As long as you need me to." Confident, not arrogant.

She just might be in love.

For the next two hours she drew him, moving him to a new position about every third or fourth drawing. She concentrated on his face and his posture. When she asked him to take off the jacket, he'd lifted both eyebrows.

"Is that an order?"

A delicious shiver of pleasure uncurled in her belly at the challenge. Her mouth dried and she flicked her tongue over her lips, desperate to moisten them.

"Yes?" The question mark punctuating the word didn't sound as confident.

"Then make it one."

A second finger of heat stroked through her. Biting down on her lip, she glanced at the profile on the paper. It was probably the best she'd done in years, and she still hadn't quite captured the pure masculine beauty standing in front of her.

"Take the jacket off." She swallowed the please.

"Yes, sir." The words reflected humor that didn't crease his lips reminding her that she'd told him not to smile earlier.

And he hadn't.

He stripped off the jacket. The white cotton stretched hard against thick biceps as he hung it neatly off the back of a chair just a foot away. He took his position again.

Did she dare?

"Take the shirt off, too." Her voice squeaked at the end, all the oxygen rushing out.

The barest hint of amusement curled the corners of his lips, but relaxed immediately and he nodded. Approval gleamed in his eyes as he stared right at her, his fingers loosening the buttons down his glorious chest. He tugged the shirt out of his pants and peeled it off, folding it like the jacket before setting it down.

The smooth bronze expanse of his wonderfully broad chest captivated her. Sinewy muscle stretched tightly under the bare skin and tapered down to his packed abdomen. Every gesture elicited a ripple of muscle.

Heat flushed her skin, but his nipples were erect and stiff against his broad chest. Exhaling a slow breath, she flipped the page of the sketchbook and didn't take her eyes off him as she began to work.

Broad chest.

Broad shoulders.

His shoulders bunched despite his relaxed stance.

The corrugated ripple of his abdomen was in sharp definition and contrast of his lean hips. But his jeans were in the way and she was already flipping to the next page, concentrating on sketching those abdominals, trying to split her attention between the page and his body. Flipping to a new sheet, she unlocked her legs and edged up onto her knees, sliding forward to get a better look. The overhead lights enhanced the taut plane, emphasizing each abdominal as a part of the whole.

Capturing the contours was the most difficult, but also the most provocative. Without thinking, she stretched out her hand to trace the line of his abdominal to the faint curl of hair visible above the cut of his jeans. Her fingertips burned at the contact and she jerked her head up to find his heavy-lidded gaze watching her.

Somehow she'd closed the entire distance between them and touched him. Did that go beyond what he'd offered her? "How shy are you?"

"How shy do you want me to be?" His words sent a tremor of excitement racing through her.

"Not at all." She lifted hopeful brows.

"Then I'm not shy at all."

Her stomach rippled and she stroked down to the edge of the rough denim. Little shivers of electricity slid along her nerves. Her sex clenched in anticipation, an uncomfortable and exhilarating feeling. She'd long since accepted her immunity to even the loveliest of men. "Then take these off."

His fingers drifted to the button of his fly and she considered moving away, but the hell of it was, she didn't want to. She wanted to see every inch of skin as it was revealed. Meeting his eyes, she said, "Now, Marine."

"Yes, sir."

The rasp of his zipper echoed loudly to her ears. The man wore neither boxer nor briefs. Her panties soaked through and she swallowed a little moaning sound because the sharp, sinewy definition popped in his thighs.

The experience of lascivious thoughts riding side-by-side with her artistic fascination struck her as surreal, but she enjoyed it. Brody simply exuded pure masculinity.

Chapter Five

The studio's chilly air glided over his skin, but he barely noticed it. Somewhere between arriving at the studio and starting to sketch, Shannon's eyes had filled with passion. Her scorching looks raked over him hotter than a desert sun.

He folded his jeans in half and set them with the shirt and jacket. He slid his shoes under the chair and scooped up the socks to roll neatly before depositing them with the rest. Shannon still knelt at the edge of the spot she'd directed him too, so he resumed a relaxed attention stance. His cock stretched and thickened lazily under her heated gaze, and his balls tightened.

But she was in charge, so he would stand for hours if needed. The rapt appreciation in her attention added more tinder to the fire beginning the slow burn inside of him.

"I...wow...um...just like that." Her breathy little whispers popped with feeling, and she split her attention between him and the sketchpad. Her pencils whispered across the page, scratching noises filling the air. She shuttled sideways on her knees to circle to his side.

She pointed a finger at him. "Eyes front."

Swallowing the laughter the demure little order tickled inside of him, he focused on her worktable. Different blocks of stone and marble rested in piles. Some looked like debris, but he could see the beginning of a shape in one. Awareness of her flared along his nerve endings as she moved behind him.

It was harder to remain still with the soft feminine scent drifting around him. The subtle scent of apples and spring rain teased his nostrils. The artist girl next door, she mixed two stereotypes into a beautiful blend. Her unease and confession drew out the need to pound some idiot college kid flat. Sadly, the kid probably didn't even realize what he'd done because it was all about a good time in college.

He subtly shifted his stance, tipping his head to the right, relieving the pull on his back and spine. Shannon entered his periphery again. Her pencil flew over the page, her lips parted, pink tongue peeking out as she focused. He'd never been the object of such intense scrutiny. It was at once both a turn on and mildly disconcerting.

"Can you twist a little more toward me?" She hesitated, the question tripping over a little catch in her voice.

"Is that an order?" He nudged her. She may have signed up for a 1Night Stand because she thought sex would reawaken the passion in her work, but it wasn't sex she needed. It was control. Control she'd lost those years ago. He'd debated the validity of PTSD with James on many an occasion and the doc had a lot of good information, but one key fact seemed to be present in every victim.

Powerlessness.

The loss of control was the hardest to reclaim. So if he did nothing else tonight, he would give Shannon her power back. She'd grabbed at it with both hands earlier when she'd ordered him to shed the denim.

She cleared her throat. "Yes, that's an order."

"Doesn't sound like an order," he teased, looking sideways at her. Her face was flushed a deep pink and her amber eyes shined.

"Twist toward me, Marine. Hands loose at your sides, feet forward, chin dipped a fraction."

"Yes, sir," he murmured. His cock strained. Who knew a woman giving him orders would be such a turn on? He didn't mind the position. It put her in his direct line of sight. Her stiffened nipples clearly tented the shirt she wore, the cotton clinging to the pebbled skin.

His balls squeezed. She wasn't wearing a bra.

He approved.

"Better?" He tested the limits of what she was going to tell him to do.

"Yes." She breathed out the word and even the tips of her ears reddened where they peeked out from the black mass of hair piled up in curls. He wondered what it would be like to strip the pins out and let that magnificent length of hair fall. "Do you want to see?"

Hell yes he wanted to see, but it was probably just the sketch she was offering. "Please."

Air brushed against him as she rose to her feet and held out the sketchpad. She'd filled a dozen pages easily. She'd sketched his face, his chest, his shoulders, a length of his thigh and to his own amusement, his ass. She'd drawn three pages of his ass.

"You have the most amazing definition. I can see every muscle group clearly." She mimed shaping his chest in the air. "I can't wait to get my hands wet and start work."

His cock bobbed its approval. Of course, it had to be her call. Her order. If she didn't demand it, he and his enthusiastic cock would be shipping out of her studio in a few hours. He tamped down the desire to push for more right then and grinned at her.

"You're really talented."

"Thank you." She looked up, the blush stained her cheeks to pure pink. She wore next to nothing in makeup, scrubbed fresh and bright eyed. A contrast to the nervous woman fighting to keep her hands around her coffee cup, but far closer to the sultry voice she'd adopted when translating the song.

He could spend weeks delving into every layer of this woman. He wanted to know every facet of her personality. He ached to explore every inch of her slender, compact body with its aroused nipples teasing him through her shirt.

Slow down, Marine.

The internal order did little to quench the thirst developing for a particular drink of the cool, endless water he imagined on her parted lips.

"Do you mind if I touch you?"

Hardly. But he didn't give voice to the thought. "That's up to you. You're in control, remember? You decide."

She sucked her lower lip between her teeth the way he wanted to, but he remained still.

"That doesn't seem fair to you." Her voice quavered on every word. "I mean, you're naked and I'm not. I'm drawing you and you're just standing there."

"I don't mind. I like the way you look at me." *I'd like it even better if you touched me, so seize that brass ring, woman. I'll catch you.* But he kept that thought to himself. He could only give her so much control and she had to take the rest. Reclaim her power and wield it.

He was more than willing to let her wield it over him.

"Lieutenant...."

"Seriously? My name is Brody." He gave her a stern look. "I'm right here, Shannon. You can do what you want. You don't have to do anything but make sketches. You're the one in control."

"But doesn't that take away your ability to choose?" She swayed away from him and then back, each motion inching her closer to him.

"Only if I didn't want to give that power to you." He sighed. Maybe he was going about it the wrong way. Maybe it wasn't enough to tell her she had the power, to encourage her to take it, but showing her might scare her more. "Look at me, Shannon. Look at all of me."

He watched her eyes dip, the heat of her gaze scorching his skin. She fixated on his chest. Her expression betrayed the struggle against looking lower, but she won and her audible inhale encouraged him. She circled until she stood less than a foot away, staring at his fully engorged dick. Swollen to the point of discomfort, he didn't think it could be any clearer that he was all in.

Her hand eased forward and Brody forced every muscle to rigid stillness. His cock jerked in anticipation of the first brush of air preceding her fingers. She drew one over the tip and it beaded with pre-cum. His body didn't give a damn about his good intentions.

You can do this, Shannon. Trust me. You can do this. The thoughts filled with encouragement barely drowned out the roar of need racing through his blood. It was a hell of a good thing he was there and not Matt. The younger Marine wouldn't have had it in him to take care of her. Brody ignored the irrational flare of jealousy thinking about the kid being there instead of him.

Matt wasn't. Brody was. End of story.

"I want to do more, but I am not even sure how to start, so...." Her hesitation tightened the pressure on his scrotum, but he waited patiently while her finger stroked the line of his cock to the base and up again.

"Help me." The quaver in her voice didn't sound like an order. She sucked in a noisy breath then exhaled roughly. "Show me how to do this, Marine. Take my clothes off and show me how to touch you."

Now, *that* was an order.

Hallelujah.

Shannon's body pulsed with arousal, fear, uncertainty, and a desperate longing she could barely identify. She'd run away from intimate situations before, fled from them as though the devil himself rode at her heels. She'd signed up for a recovery class, attended therapy sessions, and read dozens of books on the subject. She'd even allowed two artist friends to try and make love to her, but their touch left her cold, alone, and uncomfortable. But not Brody.

God, not Brody.

He touched her with his gaze in a way that seemed to caress her soul—from that first moment in the club when he reacted to the music, to the approval in his eyes when she'd told him to strip. He reacted to her, but he didn't treat her like a victim.

The rational part of her mind acknowledged that he was seducing her. Surrender and seduction weren't mutually exclusive, but the challenge of having this strong man surrender to her will was overwhelming. She could do what she wanted to do, but beyond studying his beautifully sculpted body and the fervent desire to lick him up one side and down the other, she didn't know what to do.

Worse, she didn't know how to communicate that need. Rational thought dissolved with the need to take what the man in front of her was offering. If she knew how, she'd already be wrapping her body around him and begging him to drive that fierce, thick cock into her.

But she did know how. Didn't she?

Is that an order? His voice whispered seductively in her mind, trailing lazy tendrils of desire through the ribbons of thought.

She didn't know how to do it, but he did.

"Help me." Dammit, she sounded so weak. She forced a long breath and banished her fear with the exhale. She could do this. She could drag the control away from him and surrender to it at the same time. "Show me how to do this Marine, take my clothes off and show me how to touch you."

His smile grew and every muscle in her body tensed. Triumph and pride filled his eyes and he reached out to tug her shirt from her pants. He took his time and his fingers grazed her bare sides.

She forgot how to breathe. Emotion fisted around her heart, it wasn't only lust, but it certainly tasted like it. She'd almost forgotten how the wild, rampant tingles could pierce through her reserve. He urged her arms upward, his gaze never leaving hers. She had to pull her hands away from the swollen heat of his cock and the damp, flushed tip.

An electric current raced through her blood as the shirt came away. She stood, bare-chested and vulnerable to his gaze. She'd always thought herself small compared to other women. She didn't think she'd enjoy being nude, especially not with a man looking at her. But Brody was so much more than just *a man* and his attention caressed her stiffened her nipples further. The awareness that she'd captured his attention so overwhelmingly crowded through her mind.

She wanted to cover her breasts, but the very idea repulsed her so she held her arms aloft. Arousal clenched her sex tightly, but where she was hesitant, Brody was patient.

Kneeling slowly in front of her, he slid the zipper down on the side of her pants, his hands framing her hips. Thumbs hooking into waistband of the dress slacks, he peeled them down and carried her damp panties with them. He said nothing, carefully bracing her as she stepped out of the pants. He smiled, his nostrils flaring as he paused to press a kiss to her navel, just above the dark curls hiding her sex.

The feathery glide of his lips against her skin filled her mind with the most provocative images. Her imagination didn't need a lot of encouragement to feel his breath against her thighs, or the hard heat of his muscles stroking her body. Her nipples tightened, almost painfully, and she wanted to weep for the emotion sweeping through her.

The fear tumbled free, smashed by the excitement lancing through her. She wanted him to touch her. The lust gleaming in his eyes said he wanted to touch her.

He paused, almost considering. His gaze skated around the room. She didn't know what he saw when he looked at her studio with its wild variety of statues and sculptures in various states of completion.

"What are you looking for?" She couldn't quite mask the breathless anticipation in her voice or the impatience surging through her. Her sex clenched, dampness moistening her thighs. This close to such utter perfection and she was ready to explode from want.

"A bed," he murmured. "Or something that isn't filled with sharp tools that would damage your perfect skin."

Oh.

He thought she was perfect. Tears flooded her eyes and she lowered her arms slowly and held out a hand. "Come with me."

Threading her fingers with his, she pivoted slowly on one foot and half-skipped, half-danced through the shadows cast by the overhead lights. She guided him through her workspace to the room hidden by an oriental divider. She spent so much time in her studio, she'd installed a bed where she could pass out when the muse let her go. Anticipation curled through her, chasing away the sudden surge of old doubts.

The oversized double mattress was hardly big enough for Brody. The tangle of sheets was all jersey cotton and she'd forgotten to make it again. She turned toward him and he crowded into her until the back of her knees touched the edge. Pulling her hands up to his chest, he flattened her palms against the flexing muscles, guiding her hands with easy strokes, letting her fingers trace the lines of his chest. His heart beat a steady cadence and his chest rose and fell with shallow breaths.

He seemed to be as affected by their touching as she was. She swallowed convulsively, aching with so many different emotions, and she didn't know how to give voice to them all.

"Shannon?" The gentle, sweeping word teased and comforted her. The absolute gentleness carried no hint of judgment and released a wave of tenderness in her breast.

Warmth teased her skin as the length of his body pressed close to hers, not quite touching. She basked in the heat, the slow understanding, the naked desire that he made no show of hiding, or the patience that shook off the last, lingering doubt.

She wasn't that girl anymore. She had the control, it didn't matter how much he wanted her. He wasn't doing a damn thing unless she told him to do it. He'd given his pleasure into her hands and from the wide, thick size of his cock, his want was apparent. But he only stroked his body with her hands, doing exactly what she'd told him to do.

"Why not your cock?" She asked the question, blushing at the boldness obvious in her words.

"Because I'm worried that I'll come all over you if I let you stroke me."

She loved his rippling muscles beneath her fingers. She could study their shape for hours, but the easy confession of his own precarious state had her pulling her hands from his. She took his face in her hands. Despite his shaved appearance, she felt the hint of stubble on his cheeks.

Rising to her tiptoes, she guided his face down to hers and whispered, "Kiss me." Their lips brushed together, once, twice, three times and then his mouth slanted over hers, his tongue gliding in and demanding entrance. She parted her lips under his, clinging to him while their tongues tangled.

She slid her hands up to smooth over his close-cropped hair. The cut tickled and tingled against her palms. She surrendered to the need to touch him and stepped into him, electricity bloomed through her as her nipples brushed his chest and his stiff erection thrummed against her belly.

He tasted so wildly, intensely masculine that she barely noticed the undercurrents of coffee, or the light dinner they shared. All she tasted was Brody, and she moaned his name into his mouth.

The delicious moment filled her with a confidence she'd never experienced and when she broke the kiss, they both panted heavily. His eyelids were lowered, drowsy with passion, and his firm lips curved into the sexiest smile.

"Make love to me," she beckoned. "Touch me."

Brody held onto his control by the thinnest of strings. Watching her take back her own power through control was the most arousing thing he'd ever experienced. Imagining his cock sliding into the vise of her sex had him on the cusp of blowing. He wasn't kidding when he said he wasn't sure he could hold out against the stroke of her fingers, not after nearly losing it to the single brush of her fingertip along his head.

But this wasn't about him. He'd given the entire night to her and his pleasure stoked hotter because of the woman blooming in his arms. She tasted of coffee, sweet cinnamon, and a spice so feminine that it provoked every male instinct he had to claim her.

The rapid beat of her pulse, the quiver in her words, even the hesitation in her smoldering eyes told him that as titillated as she was, the power he gave her was as frightening as it was intoxicating. So she was giving it back, through her orders.

Brody slid his hands down to cup her sweet little ass and then he lifted her, driving himself crazy by stroking her body up the length of his. He deposited her on the bed, following her down and catching himself on one arm. He teased the line of her jaw and then swept down to one breast, sucking the hard little nipple into his mouth.

Her skin was a wild contrast of petal softness and pebbled hardness. Her fingers clutched his head, but he refused to hurry. He transferred his attention to her other breast, teasing the hard little nipple with light grazes of his teeth until she began to roll underneath him. His body throbbed, begging him to bury himself in the sweet, little sex. He traced his lips down her belly, pressing a kiss to the ridge of curls before delving deeper.

She was wet with need and the musk of it filled his mind with erotic images of hot, wet, mind-blowing sex. Wildness filled him along with the urge to flip her over and pound out the desperate need for release crawling through him. He wanted to pick her up and settle her on his cock and encourage her to ride him into oblivion.

He wanted to slam her against a wall.

He wanted to take her on the floor.

Every position flashed through his mind as his fingers parted her damp lips, and the heady scent of her arousal filled his lungs. She rose up to her elbows, her mouth parted as she stared at him. Their eyes met and he leaned forward to draw his tongue up the length of her slit.

Her head fell back and she cried out, the response so raw, naked and primal, he refused to tease her any further. She wanted him to make love to her. Pushing a hand under each thigh, he pressed her wider so he could delve his tongue between the folds.

Her muscles clamped, flexing and pushing back at him, but he held her firm and took her sweet little clit into his mouth. She moved under his mouth, her ass grinding against the bed. Three firm flicks of his tongue and she exploded. He drew away, slipping his finger along the labia until he could stroke her clit gently, petting her through the orgasm. He drank in the image of her, her curls tumbling free as her head rubbed against the sheets.

As she finally stilled and looked up at him, her amber eyes warm with release and passion, he slid his finger away and put it to his lips. She tasted so fucking sweet. Her mouth opened and he saw the tension beginning to coil in her. She reached out, but he evaded, backing up quickly to dart into the other room. He'd never moved so fast in his life when he grabbed his jeans and jerked a condom from the pocket.

He was back in record time, unrolling the latex over his aching cock. She was up on her elbows, her face softening at his return. He wasted no time in covering her orgasm-loose body with his. He dove down to capture the smile on her lips in a kiss. She responded, her tongue gliding out to meet his. The abandon with which she gripped him was his undoing. Shannon had no idea what control she really had over him, and he realized it only in the moment that his patience snapped.

He devoured her mouth, shifting his hands down to lift her hips, positioning her. He broke the kiss and grasped his cock to guide it to her slick entrance and pressed forward slowly. Desire flooded her expression and she dug her fingers into his shoulders. But she didn't close her eyes as he pushed his way into the silken, hot glove of her sex, the muscles clenching him so fiercely he thought he would explode.

She was so damn tight.

Inch by inch, he worked into her sex. Because no matter what her experiences were before, she was tighter than any virgin he'd ever had the pleasure of tasting, and they all paled in comparison to the wild, wanton rising to meet him. She nodded her head as though giving him the assent he needed. Bracing her hips, he pulled back and thrust in, deeper and deeper. Her legs rose to lock around him.

He wanted to make it last, but his body had other ideas, especially when she thrashed up to meet him, pelvis to pelvis and stroke for stroke.. His balls drew tight and when she let out a moan that carried his name, he jerked convulsively against the hard fisting of her sex around him.

The orgasm shredded him and he collapsed slowly, careful to not crush her and then rolled, pulling her boneless, trembling body on top of him. They tangled in the sheets and the musky scent of their passion. She lifted her head drowsily and looked down at him, an almost heathen-like smile.

"How long before I can order you to do that again?"

Brody laughed.

Epilogue

Six Months Later
Somewhere in the Middle East

"*L*ieutenant, mail call." The private dropped a small bundle on his belly and ducked back out of the dimly lit room without waiting for a response. The dry heat of the day permeated the sandstone building and if he didn't have night patrols to run, he wouldn't even be in his bunk. Picking up the little bundle, he stared at the return address.

Shannon.

He grinned. The sexy little artist had turned out to be a hellion in bed. He'd spent most of his leave going back and forth between Mike's Place and her studio. They talked. They had sex. They talked some more. And he posed for her.

When his leave was up, the hardest part had been saying goodbye. Harder still was her driving him to the airport and standing there with that wobbling smile. She didn't cry, but he'd seen the glimmer of tears in her eyes. It was the first time anyone had been there to see him off and it unraveled a fierce emotion in his chest.

He forgave the guys in that moment. Forgave them for setting him up, a confession he'd wrung out of Damon after admitting he was crazy about Shannon, but didn't want to tell her that he'd been a stand in. Apparently, they'd signed him up for Madame Eve's 1Night Stand, but didn't think he'd go for it. Matt, it seemed, volunteered for the ruse and he'd fallen for it.

Thank God, I did.

Touching the envelope to his nose, he could imagine it perfumed with Shannon's elusive spice. She wrote him religiously, mostly about her work and how excited she was. She filled every letter with so many details. He could see her working away in her studio. She was going back to Italy in three months and he had leave coming.

He was going to meet her in Florence.

Tearing the envelope open carefully, he caught the photo that fell out. The writing on the back was in Shannon's curly, artistic scrawl and it just said, "My Marine."

Flipping it over, he grinned.

The statue stood brazenly in the center of her studio. The man's rugged features were definitely Brody's. But it wasn't just the raw naked man, but the mirror formed from dark marble that reflected a saluting Marine, field gear and all, facing the nude that undid him.

Damn right, I'm her Marine.

Semper fi.

~ABOUT THE AUTHOR~

Heather Long lives in Texas with her family and their menagerie of animals. As a child, Heather skipped picture books and enjoyed the Harlequin romance novels by Penny Jordan and Nora Roberts that her grandmother read to her. Heather believes that laughter is as important to life as breathing and that the Easter Bunny, the Tooth Fairy and Santa Claus are very real. In the meanwhile, she is hard at work on her next novel.

You can visit Heather online at:
www.heatherlong.net

Still craving Marines?

She's one of the few…

Jazz has been one of the guys for over a decade, serving her country with distinction, but she longs to explore her femininity, to be desired as a woman, to flirt, cavort and fulfill every sexual desire. When her mother of all people, signs her up for a 1Night Stand, she's not sure whether to be exhilarated or pissed. Flying to Las Vegas on the promise of a total escape, Jazz plans to be Jasmine for just one night, because tomorrow, she plans to re-up for another five years?

They're two of the proud…

Logan Cavanaugh grew up across the street from his best friend and brother-in-arms, Zach Evans. Inseparable, the two have shared everything, including women, until the year before when an IED attack during combat injured both of them. Zach suffered a concussion, but Logan's injuries were far more extensive. After a year of physical therapy, he can walk, but he'll never run or love a woman again, or so he fears. He's ready to accept his impotence, but Zach has other ideas. He hopes a 1Night Stand date with the perfect woman will heal Logan's confidence and masculinity?

They're all Marines…

They'll share each other, but will one night be enough?

Decadent Publishing Company
www.decadentpublishing.com